The Northrop Mystery
[THE BOLT]

An almost true story

R. J. Pennington

 New Generation Publishing

DEDICATION

In memory
of
Norma,
My childhood friend
who tragically, died
aged nine.

ACKNOWLEDGEMENTS

With grateful thanks to my next door neighbours, Philip and Catherine Ingram. When I told Catherine that I was thinking of writing a murder mystery, she told Philip, and he went and got me an old computer. Catherine then showed me how to use it. Further more, Catherine, on numerous occasions when I was stuck, with my computer came into my home and helped me out.

My son, Lloyd Pennington, listened to my plot over the telephone, saying, "Well, that is a good story, Dad, if I was you, I would write it. He also built me a computer when my old computer wasn't compatible with my new printer.

My lady friend, Charmian Coates, BA Hons in Creative Writing, did a lot of typing for me and put ideas my way, which I consider vastly improved The Northrop Mystery.

Charmian's granddaughter, Sarah, came and tried to help me quite a few times with the laptop which was very good of her.

ABOUT THE AUTHOR

This is R.J.Pennington's first novel. He was the youngest of three children, and was born in 1943 at Number 8, Wood Lane, Wrightington Bar. He has three children, eight grandchildren, and one great-grandson.

His ambition as a boy was to be a detective after reading a book on detectives and their work.

This novel reflects his early ambition. One of the things he did to pretend he was a detective was to go to a chemist and ask for Hydrargyrum cum creta. The chemist asked him what it was for. He replied, to reveal latent fingerprints. The chemist then said, "I can't let you have it. It contains Metallic Mercury, a deadly poison!" So he went home and had to be satisfied with talcum powder.

An earlier experience that helped him to think as a criminal was when he cut an inch and a half off the handle of his dad's new small paintbrush. This was to be used as the trigger for a wooden 17th century flintlock pistol he was making. He threw the remains of the paintbrush behind some empty jam jars that were on an old dressing table in the shed. This his father later found. He then got a hiding from Dad's leather belt. This taught him two valuable lessons; the first one was not to cut up a good item to make something else from it. The second, and most important lesson, was to **get rid of the evidence!**

The reason he couldn't realise his ambition to be a detective was that a policeman had to be a minimum height of 5' 9" at that time, and he didn't attain this height. So he ended up leaving school at 15, and working in a textile mill rising to Overlooker, until the closure, of the mill in 1980.

CONTENTS

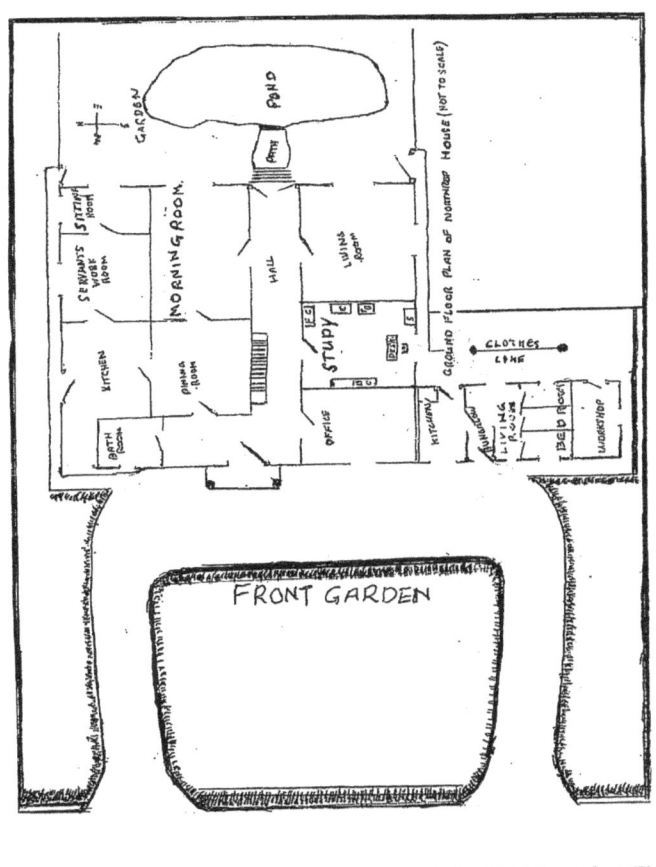

GROUND FLOOR PLAN OF NORTHIFF HOUSE (NOT TO SCALE)

GARDEN

POND

PATIO

MORNING ROOM

SITTING ROOM

SERVANTS WORK ROOM

KITCHEN

DINING ROOM

BATH ROOM

HALL

STUDY

OFFICE

LIVING ROOM

KITCHEN

CLOTHES LINE

LIVING ROOM

BED ROOM

WORKSHOP

FRONT GARDEN

CARRHOUSE LANE

9

PROLOGUE: A Brief History

Seven miles north of the town of Wigan, Lancashire, now Greater Manchester lay the sleepy village of Wrightington. Nothing exciting ever happens in Wrightington, except in 1943 when I was born and again in 1958, when this story takes place. It seems that the recent history of the Northrop family had been dogged by misfortune at least, or worse still by a curse.

The Northrop's made their family fortune in the iron industry during the 1800s by William Northrop, Brett Northrop's Great grandfather. He started work in a blacksmith's shop when he was only twelve years old.

William was a quick learner and a hard worker, and at fourteen he was made an apprentice to Joseph Lang. By the time he had reached the age of nineteen, he had taken over the forge from Joseph who was retiring aged seventy-eight having no children of his own. William had taken on the job of doing small iron castings and never looked back; going from strength to strength he built up the foundry into a thriving business.

William's only son Henry had inherited the iron foundry on the death of his father.

The circumstances surrounding Henry's death was somewhat arcane. He had apparently committed suicide. Henry's wife had been found dead in a pool of blood having been struck several times over the head with a blunt instrument. One of Henry's 'bloodstained' hammers had been discovered in the foundry, and a verdict of murder was brought in at the inquest, against Henry.

Suicide whilst the balance of his mind was disturbed was the verdict returned on Henry himself.

Although, of the people who knew Henry there were those who said that he was incapable of doing such a thing and that a third party was involved. So the truth about the death of Henry's wife and that of Henry himself remains a mystery. And as it is often said, history repeats itself.

Henry had bequeathed the foundry to his son Nathan, and Nathan's twin sister, Mary. Unfortunately Mary had died, unmarried at the tender age of seventeen, while giving birth to a baby boy, John, on the 15th of April 1912, the very day that the Titanic had sank. The boy's paternal grandparents had brought him up, and at fourteen years of age in 1926 he began work at the foundry. Mary's brother, Nathan, Brett's father managed the foundry until his untimely death at the age of fifty. He and his wife, Frances were walking to church one Sunday, as they always did, when a sudden storm blew up. Whilst they were sheltering under an old oak, the tree was struck by lightning, killing both of them. All very bizarre indeed, even uncanny! Brett and his younger brother, Peter had inherited the family business, at that time, but Peter had met Christine, a Canadian girl, whilst she was studying at university in England, and had emigrated from England to Canada leaving the foundry in Brett's hands.

Meanwhile Peter had married Christine Day, the only child of widower, Christopher Day who owned a lumber/timber firm in British Columbia in western Canada, and had made his son-in-law, Peter, his partner in the business.

Sadly, within a few years of the marriage Christine and her father were killed, in a tragic car accident under suspicious circumstances [which were never proven because of insufficient evidence] a front wheel had come off the car in which they were travelling and the car had plunged into a ravine, Christine and her father had died instantly, and as there were no children from the marriage, Peter had been left all alone.

Wrightington is not a compact little village but a sprawling place with farms, and houses, churches, and pubs dotted about. It even has a hospital famous for pioneering, hip replacement surgery. But the part of the village we are concerned with here is an area known as Wrightington Bar. I was born at No. 8 Wood Lane, opposite the Scarisbrick Hotel, behind which is Carr House Lane where Northrop House stands.

The house itself had been built in about three acres of land and has a driveway to the front, more or less in the shape of a horseshoe, with an entrance at either end with well maintained lawns and garden, and at the rear of the house, a large lawn with flowerbeds and borders, with an ornamental pond in the centre. The building was made in a red coloured brick with the later addition of a small bungalow and combined workshop to the right hand side.

CHAPTER ONE
The Lost Key

It was eleven thirty am on a gloriously sunny summer day when Brett Northrop unlocked his study door and entering the room, turned and locked the door behind him, which was not, an unusual thing for him to do.

The room was furnished with a few good quality items, Brett's: oak desk and chair in green leather with its back to the window, moving around the room in a clockwise direction, on the left, an oak bookcase; in the wall opposite the window, was the door through which Brett had entered the room leading out to the L shaped hall, and a filing cabinet, along the wall to the right, a cupboard, with double doors, also in oak, and a tallboy. To the right of Brett's chair by the window stood a safe.

Brett went and sat down at his desk; he picked up his fountain pen and began to write... *nothing.* "Empty," he muttered to himself. Flipping open the top of his ink well, he dipped the nib of the pen into the ink and pulled up at the lever, the pen slipped from his fingers and shot across the desk taking the ink well with it. "DAMN," he muttered as the ink formed a small river on his desk. He grabbed the waste paper basket, which was about quarter full and emptied the contents, into the river of ink. He mopped up the spillage with the waste paper and wiped the desk dry with some tissue. By now Brett's hands were full of blue ink but fortunately, due to the high quality of the French polish and many layers of wax built up over the years, the desk was unmarked.

He walked over to the door, unlocked and opened it and went out into the hall, pulling the door closed behind him. Turning left; he walked down the hall, then turning right, he went straight to the bathroom to wash the ink from his hands.

Seven-year-old, Oliver Johnson was just coming out from the Morning Room, carrying his model yacht. He walked down the hallway towards Brett's study. On reaching the study door, Oliver grasped the door handle and without knocking, he pushed open the door, "Uncle Brett," he cried out in an excited little voice.

There was no one there. Oliver looked all around the room but his Uncle Brett was nowhere to be seen.

Oliver turned towards the door to go out, when he saw a length of fine chain hanging from the key, which was in the lock, "An anchor," he cried out. Grasping the key with his free hand he wrenched it from the lock. Leaving the study, he turned right and walked back down the hall the way he had come, taking the key with him. Oliver walked on past the doorway leading into the Morning Room and down the hall to the door that led out into the garden, he went out down the steps and onto the lawn.

Waiting for him, down by the pond were, Diana and Angela Smith; who were two of Oliver's playmates.

"Come on, Oliver," said Diana, "where have you been?"

"Looking for Uncle Brett," said Oliver, "look, I've found an Anchor."

"It's a key!" Angela said.

Oliver ignored her. Wrapping the end of the chain around a bollard, he placed the anchor on to the deck of the yacht, adjacent to it. Oliver, leaning over put the boat into the water.

"I name this ship, The Lady Diana", declared Diana.

"It's a boat," said Angela.

Oliver pushed the boat out towards the centre of the pond. Diana found a garden cane, about seven feet long. Oliver and Diana took hold of the cane and started to thrash it about in the water. The yacht began to pitch and roll, suddenly... the boat leaped upwards, and capsized. The chain unravelled itself from the bollard, as the key fell from the deck, and sank to the bottom of the pond.

On returning from washing his hands, Brett could see that his study door was ajar. He pushed the study door open and peered inside, there was no one in. He entered the room and closing the door... stopped in his tracks, the key was not in the lock.

He instinctively thrust his hand into his pocket; no key was to be found. "Where the heck"... he broke off, and stormed out of his study. He marched down the hall and entered the Morning Room where Alice Bentham, Brett's housemaid was busy dusting.

"You haven't been into my study have you, Alice?"

"No, I haven't."

"Where's young Oliver?" asked Brett.

"He's outside playing with the Smith twins," replied Alice.

Brett went out of the Morning Room and through the outside door leading onto the lawn, where the children were playing. "Oliver, have you been into my study this morning?" he asked.

"Yes," Oliver replied sheepishly.

"Have you taken the key?"

"I'm sorry, Uncle Brett, I only borrowed it but"...

"It's at the bottom of the lake," said Diana.

"It's what!" exclaimed Brett, angrily

"Oh, oh," wailed Oliver; "a huge tidal wave came up and the boat tipped over with the key on it."

"Diana and Oliver were making waves with a big stick," said Angela.

"Pass me that cane, please, Diana."

Diana, blushing, because of her sister telling the truth about the capsizing of the yacht, picked up the cane and handed it over to Brett. He took the cane from Diana's hand and reaching out as far as he could; he just managed to catch hold of the back end of the upturned boat. He teased and tugged at the grief stricken hulk, which had become entangled with the water lilies. Gradually the boat came closer and closer to the edge of the pond, until he could finally, bend down and pick it up.

Brett looked at the yacht, but there was no sign of his key.

Brett turned to Oliver, "You come with me, Oliver, we'll go and see your dad, and you girls had better go home now, Oliver will not be playing out anymore today."

They all set off to walk around the side of the house, and along the path to the front of the house, where Oliver said his goodbyes to the girls, who walked down the drive and disappeared from view.

Brett and Oliver walked towards the bungalow, where Oliver lived with his father, Frank, who was Brett's gardener and handyman, his mother, and his crippled, grandfather, Bill. Brett knocked on the door and waited.

CHAPTER TWO
Mr. & Mrs. Johnson

Margaret Johnson, Oliver's mother opened the door, she was a good-looking young woman of about twenty-seven, and was 5'7" tall with a slim figure. She weighed about seven and a half stone, with auburn, shoulder length hair and dark brown eyes. She wore a shirtwaist dress with a floral print, and blue shoes which matched the dress. On seeing Brett, Margaret's face broke out into a broad smile; "Good morning, Brett." Just as she spoke the clock in the hall struck twelve o'clock. "Won't you come in?" asked Margaret. "I was just about to prepare lunch."

She held the door wide open, as if to encourage Brett to enter. Brett and Oliver went into the bungalow. "Have you been a good boy for Uncle Brett, Ollie?" his mother asked. Not expecting the answer she was about to get.

"I've been a naughty boy." Oliver bowed his head,

"Why? What have you done?"

"I've lost Uncle Brett's key," he replied. "I didn't mean to, Uncle Brett, it was an accident," wailed Oliver, bursting into tears.

He turned to Oliver "all right," Brett said, "Your dad may be able to find it."

Brett Northrop was not really Oliver's uncle, but Oliver had been brought up almost as if, he were Brett's son, and Oliver always had the run, of Northrop House as if it were his own home.

"Is Frank in?" asked Brett.

"He's taken his father up to Bob Trafford's for a couple of hours. He should be coming in any time now, for his lunch, Will you have some with us?"

Brett agreed to stay for some lunch. "You don't come around as often as you used to," said Margaret, with a thin smile. Brett did not answer; he had good reason, not to, for he knew that Margaret still fancied him. Margaret went into the kitchen to make the lunch.

Brett looked around the small living room. As ever, it was spotlessly clean. The woodwork of the modest furniture, shone like mirrors, the furniture comprised mainly of: a small table with four chairs, a sideboard with three drawers down the middle and a cupboard at each end. A display cabinet with glass in the sides and doors, filled with knick-knacks, and bric-a-brac. And the pale grey coloured moquette three-piece-suite, on which he was sitting. A light coloured carpet square covered most of the floor. And the tiled fireplace with the grate made up ready to light, with newspaper, sticks, and small pieces of coal on top. The room was decorated in pale primrose coloured wallpaper with blue forget-me-nots, which Brett had helped Margaret to choose.

"Frank's here now," came Margaret's voice from the kitchen. A few moments later, Frank Johnson entered the living room.

"Hello, Frank, how are you?" asked Brett.

Frank Johnson was a slim fellow about 5' 8" tall, with a thin face slightly ruddy, and a shock of black curly hair which fell onto his forehead. Although Frank was only twenty-seven, he looked more like forty. Not that he was wrinkled or anything but just had a kind of mature look about him, with his square jaw line and slightly protruding teeth.

"Lunch is ready," Margaret shouted from the kitchen, coming through with plates in her hands, she put the plates on the table, "Come on, Oliver, come to the table. You're here next to me, Brett."

They all sat down, and began to eat a delicious meal of cold chicken with a mixed salad.

"I've come to see if you can find my study key?"

"Your study key, 'ave you lost it?"

"Well, sort of."

"Oliver's lost it," said Margaret.

"'ow did you manage to lose Brett's key, Oliver?" his dad asked.

"I put it on my boat and the boat tipped over."

"It's at the bottom of the pond," said Brett. "Do you think you can find it?"

Frank did not speak but just sat there shaking his head his mouth turned down at the corners.

"That pond's not lined; it's a mud bottom. I don't think there's much chance at all, of findin' your key, the more you rummage about, the more chance you'll 'ave of buryin' it deeper, never mind findin' it," said Frank.

"Bread and butter?" asked Margaret offering the plate to Brett. "Thank you," he responded taking a slice of bread from the plate.

"I don't suppose we have a spare key, do we?" asked Brett.

"No, we 'aven't," said Frank.

"Can we get one?"

"I don't know, bein' the annual 'olidays an' all. You know the same company that made your safe, made that lock. The Pentagon Lock and Safe Company, based in London, but I think they 'ave an office in Manchester. We may 'ave to buy a complete new lock," said Frank "I won't be able to do anythin' until after the 'olidays, anyhow."

"Can you fix me up with something temporarily to lock the door with, when I am in my study, as you know; I don't like to be disturbed, when I'm working."

"I'll 'ave a look in the workshop after lunch, to see if I can find somethin' suitable." said Frank.

Brett thanked Margaret for the lunch, and said goodbye, after devouring homemade apple pie, with cream and ice-cream, Brett's favourite. "Goodbye, Oliver. Be a good boy for your mum. I'll see you tomorrow."

"Ok, I'll be good, Uncle Brett, bye," he said pushing past and running off outside. Frank and Brett went out through the back door, and went into the workshop next to the bungalow, Frank's workshop was full of all kinds of tools: the lawn mower, and other gardening tools, and an array of woodworking, and metalworking tools, part used tins of paint and all sorts of things. Frank searched in drawers, and boxes, but could not come up with anything.

Suddenly Brett said, "That's it! That will do." Holding the door closed, on a tool cupboard was a 3" brass bolt.

"I'll take it off an' polish it up," said Frank, an' I'll come round an' fit it after I've brought my dad back from Bob Trafford's."

On returning with his father from his visit to Bob's, Frank went into his workshop to polish up the bolt.

A knock on the back door brought Margaret scurrying into the kitchen. Is that Oliver up to his pranks again? she thought. On opening the door it was Alice Bentham with a letter in her hand.

"Hello, Alice, what can I do for you?"

"I have a letter for you; John asked if I would bring it round, it must have been put through the letterbox with the house mail by mistake."

"Oh, thank you, won't you come in?"

"I'll just come in for a few minutes; I really have to get back to my work."

"I know what you mean, I'll have a pile of ironing to do shortly, and I haven't washed up the pots from lunchtime yet."

"Yes," Alice said thoughtfully.

Alice stayed for about five minutes and then left the way that she had come, through the back door.

Margaret put the pots into the bowl in the sink and started to wash them. Frank came in from the workshop.

"Would you do me a favour, Frank? Could you bring the washing in for me?"

"Ok, I'll bring it in for you."

As Margaret sorted through the clothes she said, "The ribbon from my white gypsy blouse is missing."

"Per'aps it's come out in the wash."

"No, it can't do, I always tie the ends together," she said.

Margaret searched through all the clothes again, checking inside of garments to see if perhaps the red ribbon had come undone and got tangled up in something. But there was no sign of it.

"Maybe it's gone down the drain," suggested Frank.

"Either that or someone has stolen it," replied Margaret.

"Surely not, who would steal a thing like that?" he said.

CHAPTER THREE
The Bolt

It was three forty five when Frank rang the front door bell at Northrop House. John Peet, Brett's secretary and general dogsbody came out of his office, and promptly opened the door. "Hello, Frank, come in."

"'ello, I've come to put a bolt on Brett's study door, is 'e in?"

"No, he's just gone out to post a letter, you've just missed him."

"Isn't that your job, John, to post letters?"

"Well, yes," said John, laughing, "But as it was such a lovely day, he said that he would post it himself. To walk off some of that delicious lunch he'd had, with you and Margaret."

"Did 'e tell you, that Oliver's lost the key to 'is study?"

"Yes," said John, "he told me just as he was going out; it's at the bottom of the pond, isn't it?"

"Yes, that's right, it is, an' gone for good, I shouldn't wonder."

Frank stood in the hall, the bathroom a few yards to his left, and John's office immediately to his right. Brett's study, being the next door along the hall, opposite the staircase leading to the floor above. Approaching the study door, with its highly polished brass handle; he opened the door and stepped inside. He looked at the lock, and he was right: The Pentagon Safe Company had made it.

24

It occurred to Frank, that he could simply exchange the lock, for one from another door, which did not require to be locked. Brett could then lock his study door with the key, which fitted that particular lock. But he dismissed the idea.

Laying his tool box down on the floor, he opened it and taking out the brass bolt, which was now gleaming bright, he screwed it to the door just above the lock.

He checked that the bolt slid smoothly into its receiver, he was very pleased with his work, and gave a wry smile. Picking up his tools and preparing to leave, he glanced around the room, apart from the telephone, some notepaper, the pen stand, and inkwell with its blue ink, on Brett's desk, and the books in the bookcase, there was not another thing on display. Everything else was locked away in drawers, the cupboard or the safe. Frank opened the door, left the study and closed the door behind him.

He popped his head round the door, of John Peet's office "I'm goin' now, John. I've put the bolt on."

"Oh, he will be pleased about that. How's your father Frank?" asked John.

"'es doin' ok, but still gets a lot of pain in 'is back; 'e's still on morphine, you know. I took'im up to Bob Trafford's for a couple of 'ours this mornin'."

"How is Bob going on, I've not seen him for quite a while?"

"Oh, Bob's all right, enjoyin' his retirement," said Frank.

"Yes," John said, "I'm just writing out the invitations for his retirement party a week on Saturday, it should be a good do, about fifteen altogether. You and Margaret will be coming, won't you?"

"Yes, we'll be 'ere."

"Well, goodbye, give my regards to Margaret, won't you," said John.

"I'll see you later," said Frank, as he went out, through the front door closing it behind him.

Stocky built, with dark hair, forty-six years old, John Peet had worked in the offices of the Northrop Foundry for the last thirty-two years. He had worked his way up through the office from tea boy to become head bookkeeper. A job that he not only loved but work that he also excelled at. About four months or so previously Brett had offered him the job of becoming his personal secretary. Working mainly at Northrop House; fewer hours for the same money, somewhat surprised by this offer he had accepted the position.

As John finished typing the last few lines of the invitations that he was doing, his mind started to wander back to his humble beginnings and how he had been brought up. The struggle that it had been for his adoptive parents to educate him. How they both had to work long hours to pay for extra tuition. Although he had finished school at fourteen years of age, his guardians had still continued to support him in this way.

He got up from behind the cluttered desk, going out from his office; he immediately went into Brett's study. He stood looking at the shiny brass bolt, taking hold of the tail, he tried the bolt, it was very smooth, that'll do very nicely, he said to himself. He left the study, and went back to his office. He was just about to enter his office; when he saw Alice coming out of the Dining Room. He watched her as she came towards him carrying her cleaning things. Alice is quite attractive he thought to himself, yes, she's very beautiful. At that moment Alice looked up and saw John, and at the same time, Norah Gray, head servant came out of the Dining Room and called out to her; and with that both women disappeared back into the Dining Room.

CHAPTER FOUR
At The Post Office

The Post Office at Mossy Lea was quite full when Brett entered.

As he waited his turn in the queue, he felt a tap on his shoulder, turning round; it was Dr. Hardman, "hello, John," said Brett, "how are you going on?"

"I'm all right. You don't know Elaine, do you? She's my granddaughter; this is Brett Northrop," said John touching Brett's arm.

"Hello, pleased to meet you," Elaine smiled, as they shook hands, "there are quite a few people in today."

"You'll be coming up to the house a week on Saturday, won't you, John? It's a get together for Bob Trafford's retirement. John Peet will be sending out invitations, you'll get one in a day or two; and bring Elaine with you."

"Thank you, I'll take you up on that," said Elaine pleasantly.

"Good, that's settled then," said Brett "so I'll see you both on the 19th, a week on Saturday about seven o'clock?"

"We'll be there," Dr. Hardman replied.

"By the way, Brett, I've got some of those sleeping tablets you were asking about in my bag, I'll give them to you while you are here."

It was Brett's turn to be served, he handed the letter over to the Post Master. "First class airmail, please," he said handing over the fee. The Post

Master duly stamped the letter and placed it on one side. "Thank you," Brett turned away from the counter. "Here you are," the doctor said, handing over a small white tablet box to Brett.

"Oh, thank you; Goodbye, see you on the 19th," he said to John and Elaine, as he left the Post Office.

By the time Brett arrived home it was five fifty pm. He took his latchkey from his pocket, put it in the lock and opened the door. Brett crossed the hall, went through the Dining Room and followed the delicious smell, into the kitchen.

Norah Gray, housekeeper and cook, Brett's only live-in servant was in the kitchen, she had been busy making a sponge cake, which was now in the oven.

"That smells good."

"It won't be ready for another ten minutes yet, then it won't last more than five minutes, I'll be bound," said Norah, laughing.

"You're right there, I had a good lunch with Frank and Margaret, then I walked up to the Post Office at Mossy Lea and the fresh air has made me hungry."

"Do you want a cup of tea with your cake?"

"Yes, please, Norah, I'm gagging," he replied. "I'm just going to my study for a few minutes, I'll be back shortly. Has John gone?"

"Yes, he went about five o'clock," said Norah.

Brett left the kitchen, went out through the Dining Room and across the hall, to his study.

He opened the door and stepped inside, Frank had put the bolt on. That's good, thought Brett, as he slid the bolt into the locked position, "Very good!"

Brett went back to the kitchen. "I bumped into John Hardman in the Post Office. He's bringing his granddaughter, Elaine with him, on the 19th. Do you know her? She's very beautiful."

"No, I don't know her," said Norah, "but Anthony said he wouldn't mind coming if that's all right with you."

"Oh, young Anthony, oh, I don't know about that, not young Anthony. Oh well; I suppose he can come, but only because he's your nephew. Is he still the same, into everything?"

"Yes, only a lot more so, he's twenty four now, you know."

"He's twenty four! Time flies; it doesn't seem five minutes since he was at school."

"Do you want your tea and a piece of cake now?" asked Norah.

"Yes, I'm ready for it, and make it a big piece or else!"

"Or else what?" asked Norah.

"Or else I'll have to have two pieces," laughed Brett.

"You don't change much," said Norah.

Brett took off his glasses, and rubbed his eyes. "How long have you worked here, Norah?"

"Too long; thirty years."

"Thirty years, man and boy," said Brett.

"Cheeky! You always were the cheeky one; Peter was always the quiet one."

"Oh, before I forget Norah, will you make sure Alice Bentham can help out at Bob Trafford's party?" asked Brett.

"Yes, I'm sure she will; she said she feels a lot better since Dr. Hardman put her on insulin injections, she has to inject herself twice a day. But she says she's coping with it all right."

"That's good news," said Brett, thoughtfully.

"I'll be going up to Alice's later on, I'll check with her then, do you want anything more tonight?" asked Norah.

"No, I don't think so; I'll do a couple of hours work for tomorrow. I have some men in over the holidays, doing maintenance work while the foundry's closed. I may be down there for some time, I'll ring you if I need anything, and you can just leave me a plate of sandwiches."

"Will Sandra be working?" Norah asked with a wry smile.

"She might be."

"You know you're playing with fire there, don't you!"

Brett shrugged his shoulders, but he did not answer.

"It's time you found a nice eligible girl and settled down."

"Not me, I'm a confirmed bachelor; you know that, Norah."

"All the same, you'll get into trouble one of these days, mark my words."

"Oh, you're old fashioned, Norah."

"Yes, and that's how I intend to stay," said Norah, taking off her apron and, putting on her coat. "I'm going up to Alice Bentham's now, so think on, what I said; if you play with fire you're bound to get burned, sooner or later. Good night, I'll see you sometime tomorrow."

"Ok, I'll see you tomorrow, good night; and give my regards to Alice, will you?"

"I will, good night."

Brett went back to his study; he opened the door and went inside, closed the door behind him, and bolted it; even though there was no one else in the house.

CHAPTER FIVE
A Sad Case

It was seven fifty five am the following morning when the alarm clock started ringing.

Brett turned over and knocked off the alarm, yawning and stretching as he got up from the bed. He fumbled around on the dressing table, in the half-light, for his glasses and put them on. He went over to the window and drew back the curtains; it was another gloriously sunny day. From his window, he could see John Peet talking to Frank Johnson. "John's here already," he muttered to himself. Brett went into the en-suite bathroom for a quick shower and got dressed. He went downstairs, just in time to see John entering the front door.

"You're up bright and early," said Brett.

"Yes, I woke up early and couldn't get back to sleep so I decided to get up, and walk down here; it saves you calling for me."

"Do you want a brew before we go?" asked Brett.

"Yes, I'll have a cup of tea, one sugar," said John.

Twenty minutes later, John and Brett got into Brett's Mk.1 Jaguar, and drove the four or so, miles to the Northrop Foundry, Brett drove onto the car park, and they went in through the main front office door. It was just gone eight thirty am.

Tom Laithwaite, Brett's shop floor manager was sitting at one of the desks, "Good morning, Brett, morning John," said Tom.

"No one else here yet?" asked Brett.

"Not yet, they're coming to re-line number one furnace this morning. But that, to one side, Brett, there's a more pressing issue arisen."

"What's that?" asked Brett.

"That order from Lupton's is due after the holidays for a six ton casting; we can't afford another sad case like Bill Johnson's, you know. That cradle will have to be replaced."

The case of Bill Johnson was indeed sad. Some six years previously an overhead cradle carrying a 3 ton casting had broken, and the casting had fallen, pinning Bill between the floor and the wall crushing both his legs and breaking two vertebrae at the bottom of his back, along with other internal injuries, and cuts and bruises; which Bill was fortunate enough to survive, but he had to have both legs amputated, one above and one below the knee.

At the time, the cradle was rated at 2.5 tons, and Brett had reasoned that for a one off job, the cradle could be modified in house to handle the bigger, extra half ton casting. He had calculated that a 2.5 ton S.W.L. [safe working load] lifting device would actually carry 5 tons. However, the modification was not only illegal, but was a poorly constructed affair. Everyone, including Tom and Alan Kay had said it was an accident waiting to happen.

Bill Johnson could have successfully sued Northrop, but Brett had persuaded him to settle out of court. The deal being that Brett would have the old stables [no longer used] at Northrop House converted into a bungalow, and the garage next to it could be used as a workshop. Bill, whose wife had left him and Frank, when Frank was only three years old; and Frank and his wife, Margaret, and Oliver, who was about one year old at that time, could all live there rent free. Part of the deal also being that Frank would take on the job of gardener and handyman for which he would be paid a salary.

Bill agreed to the terms, and Frank, who was at that time studying at university to become an archaeologist; something that he had dreamt of being since he was a boy; reluctantly agreed to, but only because he loved his father so dearly, did he make that sacrifice.

During the next seven or eight months that it took Bill to recover from his injuries in hospital, Brett had the stables converted into a bungalow and Frank and Margaret moved in, along with young Oliver. Brett had given notice to his previous gardener/handyman, Harry Carter, who had worked at Northrop House for the past 30 years, and Frank took over the job.

The door of the main office opened, and in walked Sandra Kay, Brett's office secretary with her dog, Rex, a golden Labrador that had been off colour a bit lately.

"Good morning, Sandra" said Brett. "How's old slobber chops this morning?"

"Rex? He's all right," she said.

"Oh, I meant you."

"Cheeky thing," She turned, "Good morning, Tom, John," said Sandra.

"Is Alan here, Sandra?" asked Tom.

"Yes, he's downstairs, he went straight onto the shop floor."

"Well, Brett, what about that cradle, have we to go ahead with it?" asked Tom.

"Yes, go and see Alan about getting it sorted out and tell him to spare no expense, it will have to be done."

"That's good; are you coming with me, John?" asked Tom, and with that they both went out through the door that led down to the foundry shop floor.

Sandra went over to Brett, "I'll give you, slobber chops," she said.

"Ooh, when?"

"Never you mind, when," said Sandra with a broad grin on her face. [Brett could always make her laugh.] "In front of Tom and John, I don't want everybody to know what's going on, Alan already suspects something, and if they go and say something to him, what then?"

"You don't love Alan!" said Brett.

"You know who I love!" She threw her arms around Brett and kissed him.

Rex began to growl, and then he started to bark. "He's jealous," said Brett.

"Hush, Rex; he's guarding Me," said Sandra.

The hustle and bustle of the shop floor was somewhat quieted; because of the holidays; only the sound of the tapping of mallets on fire brick, and voices with the occasional shout could be heard.

In Alan Kay's office, Tom Laithwaite was telling Alan that Brett had given the go ahead for the new lifting cradle to be ordered.

"Well, now, that's saying something good at last; isn't it?" remarked Alan.

"Yes, well, thank God for that," said Tom, "I'll leave it in your capable hands, Alan; and Brett said to spare no expense."

"Well, he would do, wouldn't he, after what happened to Bill, ok, leave it with me, I'll see to it," said Alan.

"Are you and Sandra coming to Bob Trafford's retirement party?" asked John.

"Yes, we'll be there; you'll be going to Bob's do, won't you, Tom?" asked Alan.

"Yes," said Tom, "a week on Saturday, isn't it."

"It is; the 19th, you'll get your official invitations in a day or two, I posted them yesterday," John said.

"If you'd been in charge, Tom, instead of Bob, when Bill got hurt, the accident would never have happened; Bob would never stand up to Brett, whatever Brett said, Bob would always agree to, even if he thought that Brett was wrong," Alan said.

"Yes, well, it's all in the past now, Alan, and we can't turn the clock back, can we? All we can do is to learn from previous mistakes and see that they don't happen again," said Tom. Just then the shrill sound of a whistle blew for the mid-morning break.

CHAPTER SIX
It's A Small World

The number 113 bus which ran every hour on the hour, from Preston to Wigan, was running five minutes late. Norah looked at her watch, it was five minutes past one and Norah was going up to Standish to see her sister, Jane. Norah made this journey every other Thursday as a rule. Today however, she had a special reason for going to see her sister. Anthony, her nephew would be at his mother's and she could tell him that he was invited to the party at Northrop House.

Norah got off the bus at the Wheat Sheaf, and walked the short distance into High Street. She had just crossed over the road when she saw Dr. Hardman coming out of the chemist shop,

"Good afternoon, Doctor Hardman," she said.

"Good afternoon, Norah, how are you keeping these days?"

"Oh, I'm fine, and you, are you all right?"

"Yes, I'm all right, thanks."

"Brett was telling me that you're coming to Bob Trafford's retirement party on the 19th and bringing your granddaughter with you, is that right?"

"Yes, that's right; I don't think you know Elaine, do you?"

"No, I've never met her."

"Oh, you'll like Elaine, she's a trainee solicitor you know; she works for A.J. Jones and Co. in

Wigan. You know, they're in the Bank Chambers in Wallgate."

"Oh yes, I know where you mean, next to the Post Office; I'm just going to my sister's, to tell my nephew, Anthony, that he has been invited to the party, too."

"Oh, that's good! I've just been into the chemist to stock up on a few medicines and drugs."

"Speaking of drugs," said Norah, "Alice Bentham is doing a lot better since you put her on insulin."

"Yes, she said she is feeling much better; I've picked up some more insulin just now," Dr.Hardman said.

"Well, I had better get off, to our Jane's; the bus was running five minutes late, she'll think I'm not coming, I'll see you later, Dr. Hardman."

"Yes, I had better be getting a move on, too; my afternoon surgery starts in five minutes. I had better get across the road while the traffic is still slack. I'll see you a week on Saturday, Norah; goodbye, give my regards to Brett, won't you."

"Yes, I will, goodbye," said Norah; and with that she turned and walked off up the High Street towards her sister's house.

It was just gone one thirty, when Norah reached her sister's house. Jane was waiting for her at the front door. "I had almost given you up, the bus went past about five minutes ago."

"The bus was running five minutes late, and then I bumped into Dr. Hardman outside the chemist's and I was chatting with him for a while."

"Well, you're here now, come in and I'll put the kettle on."

"Good! I'm parched. Are you keeping all right, Jane?" asked Norah, as she took off her coat and hung it on one of the coat hooks, behind the door.

"Yes, I'm fine".

"What time does Anthony get home today?" asked Norah.

"He shouldn't be long; he's due any time now. But you never know with Anthony. I've had to throw many a good meal away, because he hasn't come home on time," Jane said.

"Since he moved from Manchester, to the new office in Wigan, you mean?"

"Yes, he kept better time travelling thirty miles, than he does travelling three and a half miles," said Jane.

"Who did you say he works for?" Norah asked.

"He works for Sergeant and Stone, Private Investigators; he's only been at Wigan twelve weeks; as you know, but they seem to be quite impressed with his work so far, and he had good references from the agency office in Manchester, he had worked there for them for the last seven years; and only left there because this office was so close to home."

"Anthony telephoned the other day; about a quarter past five it would be, yes; John Peet had not been gone long, and I was just getting the ingredients together to make a sponge cake, when the phone rang. He wanted to know if I could get him an invitation to the party this Saturday week; well, I didn't think that he knew Bob Trafford, and when I asked him why he wanted to come to a party for someone he didn't even know? He said; oh, you will just have to wait and see, Aunt Norah. Anyway; I asked Brett, and he said it was ok for him to come."

Just then; the door latch clicked, and the door opened, "Anthony's here now," Jane said; and into the house walked; Anthony Mark Hilton.

"Well, you're on time for once, Anthony, have they sacked you?"

"No, they haven't," said Anthony indignantly. "Aunt Norah! Have I been invited?" He was all excited; almost like a school boy waiting to be given his birthday present.

"It'll cost you;" said Norah, pointing to her cheek.

Anthony placed his hands on either side of her head and planted a big kiss on his aunt's left cheek.

"Well! I'll be bound; this can only mean one thing; a girl."

Anthony blushed.

"Well, who is she?" his mother and his aunt asked at the same time.

"And how does the party at Northrop House fit into it?" Norah enquired.

"She'll be at the party," said Anthony.

"You haven't told us who she is yet," said his aunt; questioningly.

"Her name is Elaine Blake. Elaine Veronica, angel-face, gorgeous, Blake."

41

"God; he has got it bad, hasn't he, Jane?" Norah said, "She's not Dr. Hardman's granddaughter, is she?"

Anthony nodded "Yes, she is."

"How have you come to know her?" asked his mother.

"Sergeant and Stone, take on work for solicitors for: divorces, fraud, embezzlement, and such like things. We had done some work for A.J. Jones and Co. and I had to take some paperwork to their offices and that's where I met Elaine. I didn't know then, that she was Dr.Hardman's granddaughter. I could see that she was not married or engaged, as she was not wearing any rings. However, I did think that she might have a boyfriend."

"And does she?" asked his Aunt Norah.

"Well, I plucked up enough courage to ask her what she was doing this Saturday; to see if she would say that she was going out with a boyfriend."

"And..." said Norah.

"She said that she was going shopping with her mother, and then she was going with her mum to Billinge Hospital, to see a friend who has had an operation for something or other. To be honest; I wasn't really listening, my mind was on something else."

"Mmm... we know what," said Norah.

"Then I asked her what she was doing next Saturday. She said nothing that she could think of."

"So! Go on."

"Well, at that point my courage deserted me, and so I left it at that," Anthony said. "Until that is; she rang our office and asked if she could speak to me. She said that she was sorry but she had been invited to a party along with her granddad, Dr. Hardman on Saturday the 19th at Northrop House, and that she had accepted the invitation. It was after that call; that I rang you, Aunt Norah. I could not believe my luck when she said that the party was at Northrop House."

"It's a small world, isn't it?" Norah said.

"So you'll be telling her that you are also invited to the party then," his mother remarked.

"Well, I don't know yet; I might not say anything to her, and just go to the party, and pull her leg a bit."

"What do you mean, pull her leg, how?" asked Norah.

"Well, I might just say that I'm following someone; and that they have turned up at the party. I'll keep it up for a bit, and then I'll just tell her the truth."

"Yes, and she might just kill you," Norah said, laughing.

"Elaine wouldn't do that; she wouldn't kill a fly."

"Wouldn't she?" said Norah.

"What does she look like; is she pretty?" His mother asked.

"Are you kidding?" said Anthony; she's got blonde hair, blue eyes, and Cupid's bow lips.".…

"Buck teeth, broken nose, scar down one cheek," his Aunt Norah butted in, chuckling.

"Oh, Aunt Norah! I'll tell her what you've said."

"I shall quite categorically deny it." Norah said; with an air of authority.

"Come to think of it, Brett said that she was very beautiful too, when he invited her to the party."

"Well for once, I'll agree with Brett wholeheartedly," Anthony said.

"Do you want me to run you home, Aunt Norah, when you're ready?"

"No, thank you, Anthony, I always get a return ticket, it's cheaper to book return."

After tea Norah helped her sister with the washing up, and then she put on her coat ready to go and catch the five forty bus back to Wrightington Bar. She said her goodbyes to Jane and Anthony; who planted another big kiss on her cheek, "thank you very much, Aunt Norah for getting me the invitation."

"That's all right, Anthony as long as you don't forget to introduce her to me, when you come to the party."

"I will," he promised.

At that Norah walked off down High Street, across the road, turned left at the surgery and walked the short distance to the bus stop. The bus was bang on time; Norah would be back home by six o'clock.

The bus pulled up at the bus stop, outside No.10 Guild Bungalow across the road from the Scarisbrick Hotel entrance. Norah got off the bus and crossed over the road and walked down Carr

House lane. She thought to herself, as she entered the driveway of Northrop House; "I'll see if Brett wants anything if he's in, and then I will listen to the radio for an hour or two before having an early night." Norah liked to listen to repeats of Valentine Dyall 'The Man in Black', with a cup of hot cocoa before going to bed.

She had reached the front door of the house and taking the latchkey from her handbag she opened the door; and stepped inside. The house was as quiet as a graveyard.

Norah walked up to the study door, and listened, for a moment; she could hear no sound from inside. She knocked gently on the door; still no sound came from inside. Norah knocked again a little harder. She heard the click of the bolt, as it was quickly drawn back. The door was flung open and framed in the doorway was Brett.

"Oh, Brett; I didn't know if you were in or not, I've just got back from our Jane's; do you want anything?" asked Norah.

"No, I'm ok; are you all right, Norah? You look a little pale."

"Well, you made me jump when you opened the door; I thought that you weren't in. If you don't want anything more tonight I thought that I would listen to the radio for a couple of hours and then go up to bed."

"That's ok, Norah, I'll see you tomorrow, I may have gone out before John arrives in the morning; I have an appointment with David Bird for an eye test at nine fifteen," said Brett.

"I'll see you sometime tomorrow then, goodnight, Brett."

"Good night," said Brett. Brett returned to his study, and closing the door, bolted it behind him.

CHAPTER SEVEN
The Doctor Pays A Call

On the Friday morning Brett woke up at eight o'clock and was downstairs by eight fifteen. This gave him very little time to get his breakfast, and keep his nine fifteen am appointment with D.A. Bird, his ophthalmic optician.

Norah had been up since seven thirty benefiting from her early night. Brett entered the kitchen, "Good morning, Brett," said Norah.

"Good morning," replied Brett.

"What do you want for your breakfast?"

"Just some toast, and a cup of tea, please, Norah, I haven't time for anything else."

Brett hurriedly ate his breakfast; put on his coat and was gone out through the front door by eight thirty.

Moments later, Alice Bentham came in through the side door that led, from the footpath at the side of the house directly into the kitchen. Alice came in to clean every Tuesday and Friday as a rule and today being Friday, was no exception.

"Good morning, Norah, it's another lovely day," Alice said, smiling sweetly.

"You're in a good mood this morning, Alice."

"Yes, I am; I feel on top of the world since Dr. Hardman put me on insulin, I feel ten years younger, and you wouldn't believe it."

Alice Bentham not only felt ten years younger, but looked ten years younger. She had the kind of face that never seemed to age, and could easily have passed for thirty one. Her pretty face was framed in golden brown hair, with big brown eyes, and was about five foot six tall with a very trim figure.

At that moment the door bell rang several times.

"Who can that be I wonder; has John lost his key?" Norah went out of the kitchen through the Dining Room, and out into the hall and opened the front door. There on the doorstep stood a dishevelled Margaret Johnson. "Why, Margaret; whatever is the matter?" asked Norah.

"Oh, it's Oliver, I've been up all night with him. Can I use the telephone to ask the doctor to call on him? I think that he may have caught chickenpox or something."

"Certainly, Margaret, come in. Would you like me to call him for you?"

"It's all right, thank you, Norah, I'll call him myself so that I can explain to him what Oliver's like."

Just then; the door latch clicked and John Peet entered the hallway. "Hello, is everything ok?" He asked.

"Oliver's got chickenpox." Norah said. "Margaret is just sending for the doctor."

Margaret put down the telephone. "Dr. Hardman will call after he has finished his surgery, at about twelve o'clock."

John went into the kitchen, leaving Norah and Margaret talking. "Good morning, Alice; my word you look wonderful."

"Thank you, I feel wonderful. I was just telling Norah that I was feeling a lot better since I went on insulin, I feel ten years younger, and it's my birthday on Monday."

"Oh, is it, and would it be rude of me to ask how old you are?"

"No, I'll be forty one."

"Well, you don't look it, Alice," John said with a tone of sincerity in his voice.

"Thank you."

"Are you having a party?" asked John.

"No, I wasn't intending to, I had a party last year, for my fortieth."

"Are you doing anything, special for your birthday?"

"No, I've got nothing planned," she replied

"Do you like films, or the theatre? I can get tickets for 'The Merchant of Venice' at Wigan Little Theatre; or they're showing the 'The Prince and the Showgirl' at the Ritz; if you would like to come with me?"

Alice blushed, "Are you asking me out, John?"

"Yes, I think I am; think about it over the weekend and I'll call round on Monday if that's ok."

"Yes, I will think about it, thank you, John."

Brett pulled up outside of number 12 Wood Lane; it was precisely eight forty one am with his car clock. He waited patiently; and at about eight forty five Sandra appeared at her front door. She walked down her driveway and as she approached the car Brett reached over and opened the door for her. "Has Alan gone to work?" he asked.

"Yes, he went out at twenty past eight; I had to settle Rex down before I could get away."

"He's like having a child."

Sandra smiled "Yes, well, he is my baby."

"So where do you want to go to?" asked Brett as he drove off.

"You can drop me off at the shops; while you go to the Opticians. I want to buy a new dress and shoes, and perhaps a new handbag, for the party next weekend."

"I'll drop you off outside of Debenhams then, if that's ok. And I'll meet you outside of Voses restaurant at eleven forty five, is that all right?" asked Brett.

"Yes, that's fine."

By five minutes past nine Brett and Sandra were in Wigan. Brett stopped outside of the store; he took his wallet out from his inside coat pocket and handed forty pounds over to Sandra, "My treat."

"Ooh, thank you;" she leaned over, and gave him a big kiss. "I'll see you at a quarter to twelve then; cheerio."

"Bye," said Brett and he drove off; to keep his appointment at his opticians.

Dr. Hardman's Rover turned into the drive of Northrop House and stopped outside of the bungalow. Margaret opened the door just as Dr. Hardman was getting his bag out of the boot of his car.

"Good morning, Doctor, come in."

"Good morning; lovely day," said Dr.Hardman. Margaret took the doctor into Oliver's bedroom. "Sit up, Oliver, the doctor is here."

Dr.Hardman put his bag down on the bed and opened it. He looked at Oliver and took a spatula from his bag. "Open wide and put your tongue out, Oliver, say ah."

The doctor gave Oliver a good examining. "He's got German Measles!" declared Dr. Hardman. "Keep him in bed, with plenty of cold drinks. I'll give you some medicine to ward of any complications, give him half a teaspoonful twice a day, and you can give him Fennings cooling powders. He should be well in about a week. Is there anywhere I can wash my hands?"

"Yes, come through to the kitchen." Margaret led the way out of the bedroom and through the hall. Dr. Hardman placed his bag on a chair which was in the hall; and followed Margaret into the kitchen. At that moment the hall clock struck Twelve; and at the same time, Frank came in through the front door.

"Don't hesitate to call me again if any complications do arise; which are unlikely to, once you get the medicine into him."

"Thank you very much, Doctor." Shortly after this; Frank came into the kitchen. "Oliver's got German measles, Frank," said Margaret.

"The poor lad, what a shame," said Frank sympathetically.

"Don't worry, he will make a full recovery," said Dr. Hardman. "Well, I'll get a move on; I have two more patients to see. Will I see you at the party next Saturday?" he asked.

"Yes, we are going to the party," Margaret replied.

51

"Good, I'll see you a week, tomorrow then, goodbye," Dr. Hardman said, as he got into his car and drove off.

Brett and Sandra were by now in the restaurant enjoying a delicious meal of braised steak with new and roast potatoes and two veg. "Did you get everything that you wanted?" asked Brett.

"Yes, I did, and I got something for you, too."

"Oh, what is it?" Sandra picked up one of the paper bags, that she had with her and opening it, she held it up so that Brett could see into it. Brett's eyes opened wide; inside the bag there were two sets of lacy lingerie, one set in scarlet and one set in midnight blue.

"Oh, I can't wait," he said.

"Hush," said Sandra, with that broad grin on her face, "everyone's looking at us."

"Never mind that I can't wait," Brett said in a whisper.

The waitress came over to their table, "will there be anything else?" she asked.

"Do you want a sweet, Sandra?"

"I think I'll have the Pavlova, please," Sandra said.

"I'll have the apple pie with fresh cream and ice-cream please, and can we have two coffees, please." Brett settled the bill, and after drinking their coffee and smoking a cigarette,

Brett left a good tip, and he and Sandra got up and left the restaurant.

CHAPTER EIGHT
Alice's Story

On the Monday morning; following a rather uneventful weekend, or at least, events that cannot be related at this time, John Peet, was sorting through the mail that the postman had just delivered. He noticed that there was an airmail letter amongst them addressed to Brett. John picked up the letter. There was no doubt, it was from Peter. John could not contain himself; he went straight away to the kitchen.

"Look what I've got, Norah. I could be wrong, but I think that Peter might be coming over. Brett said that he might come over, and be here in time for the party."

"Well, I'll be bound; Peter, coming home," Norah said, with great joy.

"That is good news, isn't it?"

"Well, we'll know for sure, when Brett opens the letter."

"Yes, that's right, we will," said Norah; rubbing her hands together.

John took the letter along with other letters personally addressed to Brett, to Brett's study and left them on his desk. He went back to the kitchen and as he entered, Norah said to him quite casually; "its Alice's birthday today, she's forty one".

"Yes, she is; she told me on Friday. You know Alice very well, don't you, Norah?"

"I know her better than most, why?"

"Well, let's say that I was to ask her out. What do you think she'd say?"

"Is this a serious question, John?"

"Yes, it's a serious question."

"Well, I'll be bound, John Peet! Do you know I've seen you looking at Alice and wondered; I'm sure John fancies Alice, and I was right."

John's face broke out into a big smile. "So what do you think she will say?" asked John.

"What do you mean, will say? Have you already asked her?"

"Yes, I have," admitted John, "I asked her on Friday. I told her that I would call on her today to see what she has to say. What do you think?" There was silence for a moment or two, Norah was deep in thought. She turned to John and looked him straight in his eyes "Alice is a lovely girl, don't hurt her, John. She's been hurt once before about a year ago."

"Who hurt her?"

"That's for Alice to tell you if she wants to do so, not me. But to answer your question, if she's ready she'll say yes, and if she doesn't, I'll have a word with her." Norah said with a smile. "But remember what I said, don't hurt her, or you'll have me to answer to," she said, straightening her face.

"I can promise you now that I definitely would not even think of hurting Alice. I'll have some lunch and then I'll go and see her."

"Well, good luck, John, I hope that she gives you a satisfactory answer."

"Thanks, Norah; Oh, I mustn't forget to make an appointment for Brett to see his dentist, when I get back from Alice's. Remind me, will you, Norah, I might not even know what day it is never mind anything else."

"Why not do it now, before you go?" Norah asked. "And then you won't forget. You've just got time before I serve lunch."

"That's a good idea, Norah, I'll do that."

John went back to his office and looked in his address book for the telephone number, under "D" He found: Wil Cain Dentist. He picked up the telephone and dialled the number. Preston 764488 and an appointment, was made for Brett to see his dentist on Wednesday the 16th at five pm.

After lunch John set off to go up to Alice's at No. 2 Church Lane which was only a five minute walk away. On reaching Alice's house John knocked on her front door. He thought to himself as he waited, "I wonder if Alice will come out with me?" By his feet in the narrow border against the wall of the house grew some sweet smelling Lily of the Valley which, in the gentle breeze seemed to be nodding their heads in approval.

Alice opened the door, "Come in, John, I've been expecting you."

"Hello, Alice, how are you?"

"I'm fine, how are you keeping?"

"I'm ok, too," said John, although he was secretly shaking inside. "It's another lovely day, isn't; we are having a good summer this year for a change."

John followed Alice into the living room of the tiny house, just one room up and one down; with a built on kitchen and toilet at the back. "Sit down, John, would you like a brew?"

"No, thank you, I've just had lunch. Have you thought any more about what we said on Friday?" he asked, plucking up courage.

"Yes, I have been thinking about what you said."

"And?" asked John nervously.

"I... I don't know," replied Alice shyly.

"Why not?" asked John, astonished by his own abruptness. Alice looked up at him. "I'm sorry, Alice; I didn't mean to shout at you, please forgive me."

"About twelve months ago I was going out with someone, and then in February, I found out that he was seeing another woman. At first he denied it, but when I told him that he had been seen out with her, he finally had to admit the truth. So I ended the romance. I swore then at that time, that no man would ever again hurt me in that way. So you can see why I am reluctant to go out with anyone else."

"Norah knows that I have asked you out and I told her that I would never hurt you. I can promise you now, Alice that I never will. I, too, was hurt in the same sort of way, some twenty years ago, but I haven't forgotten what it was like, even after all this time. So I do understand just how you feel."

Alice looked at him, and a tear rolled down her cheek. John leaned across and with his thumb gently wiped the tear from her face. Alice nodded her head two or three times.

"Is that a yes?" he asked.

Alice looked into his eyes,

"Yes, it is," she replied.

"Oh, Alice, that's wonderful, Happy Birthday," and with that they both burst out laughing.

"Well, that's settled; where would you like to go this evening, Wigan Little Theatre, or to the Ritz, or would you like to go somewhere else?"

"I'm not very keen on Shakespeare, but I wouldn't mind going to see 'The Prince and the Showgirl'."

"That's fine; I'll pick you up at seven o'clock, if that's ok with you."

"I'll be ready, I'm quite looking forward to it, I've not been out for a while."

"I'm sure we'll both enjoy it, Alice. I'll be back at seven; I must get back to work now, I'll see you then, bye."

As promised John picked Alice up at seven o'clock. As his Singer Gazelle drew to a stop, Alice came to her front door and waved to him. She walked down her path and reached the car just as John was opening the door for her. "Hi, Alice, you look stunning."

"Well, you look very smart, too," she replied.

John turned the car around; and at the crossroads, turning right into Mossy Lea Road, headed in the direction of Wigan. As they got near to Wigan, John could not help wondering who the bastard was that had hurt such a lovely girl as Alice in that way; and he wondered if he even dare ask her.

"Tell me who was it, Alice, that hurt you?" he blurted out.

"It's all in the past now, John, let's leave it there."

"I really would like to know, who was it?"

"I can't tell you right now, perhaps later." By now they had reached the Ritz car park, so the conversation was temporarily interrupted. John and Alice went into the cinema and joined the queue in the foyer. Ten minutes later, they were settled in their seats to watch the romantic comedy, in which Marilyn Monroe starred as Elsie Marina, the Showgirl; and Laurence Olivier co-starred as Grand Duke Charles, the Prince Regent.

The film finished at ten pm and John and Alice left the cinema. "It's a lovely night, Alice, shall we leave the car on the car park and walk up to that little fish and chip restaurant in Mill Gate; do you fancy a fish and chip supper?" he asked her.

"I'd love a fish supper, thank you, John." Upon entering the restaurant, there were still two or three empty tables and so they sat down at one of them and ordered their meals. After they had left the restaurant, and were walking back to the car park, Alice said, "Thank you for a lovely evening, I've really enjoyed it."

"So does this mean that you'll go out with me again?"

"Yes," Alice replied, "why not?" and with that John took hold of her hand to which she did not object, and so they walked hand-in-hand back to the car.

As they drove home, John's thoughts turned once again to what had happened to Alice. The more he thought about it, the more he wanted to get hold of the 'so and so' and wring his bloody neck. John could not hold it back any longer he had to ask her once more.

"Please tell me, Alice, who was it that did that awful thing to you, is it someone I know?"

She took her hankie from her handbag and dabbed her eyes. There was silence for a minute or two; Alice nervously twisted the handkerchief through her fingers until her knuckles went white.

"Please, John."

"I'm sorry, Alice, I shouldn't keep asking you, I know, only the very thought of you being treated in that way..." The gloomy silence descended once more.

"All right, I'll tell you, but you must promise not to tell a soul.

"I won't tell anyone, I promise, who was it?"

"It... was Brett" Alice said, bursting into tears.

John pulled the car to an abrupt stop by the side of the road. He turned and put his arms around her. "Brett," he repeated under his breath. John drew Alice close to him. "He'll never hurt you ever again, I'll see to that," he said, as he consoled her.

As they resumed their journey the conversation continued in the same vein.

"When did you say it was that you first went out with Brett?"

"It was last July, almost twelve months ago."

"And you said that by February of this year you had ended the liaison."

"Yes, that's right, I had, why do you ask?"

"It's just that I started working at Northrop House in March this year and so that's why I didn't know anything about it."

They had by now reached the crossroads and John turned left into Church Lane and stopped the car outside of Alice's front door.

"Won't you come in for a nightcap before you go?" she asked.

John turned off the engine. "I most certainly will." He got out of the car and opened the door for her. As Alice stepped out of the car, John caught her up in his arms and kissed her tenderly. "I'll look after you from now on, no one will ever hurt you again, Alice."

They unlocked their embrace, and Alice took the key from her handbag and opened the door. They went inside and John closed the door behind them. "Sit down and I'll make a drink; what would you like?"

"I'll have a tea with one sugar, please. You don't mind if I smoke do you, Alice?"

"No, there's an ashtray on the sideboard."

He walked over to get the ashtray. Close by there were two syringes and three ampoules of insulin, one of which was partly used. John picked up one of the ampoules and looked at it closely, picking up a syringe, he looked again at them. He took them into the kitchen where Alice was making the tea. "How often do you have to use these?" he asked.

Alice looked round. "Twice a day," she replied.

"How do you go on when you're working?"

"I have some more that I keep in the servants` workroom," she said, picking up the cups and going through into the living room.

They went and sat down on the settee. "Tomorrow's Tuesday, you will be working tomorrow, won't you, Alice?"

"I'll be working as usual, why?"

"Well, I'll be able to see you without having to wait until I finish work, won't I?"

"Yes, we shall be able to see each other providing that Brett's out of the way."

"Brett won't be there, at least not all of the time, anyway, he'll be at the foundry in the morning, at least."

"Good! Anyway, let's not talk about him."

Their eyes met once more, Alice smiled at him. "You have the sweetest smile, it suits you, Alice."

"Maybe, I've got something to smile about."

"Like what?"

"You, you clown." And with that they entwined their arms around each other and kissed passionately.

CHAPTER NINE
John's Secret

Tuesday morning was rather overcast, with clusters of black clouds dotted about here and there, a change from the hot sunny days of the past week or two. John arrived at work on time, as usual. After he had been into his office to check things out and see that everything was ok, he went into the kitchen. There waiting for him was Norah, but more importantly, as he saw it, Alice was there, too.

"John! Have you heard? Peter is coming home. Brett told me last night after you'd gone home; and Alice here has just told me some more good news. You two together, at last, well, I'll be bound and I knew it all along."

"Good morning, Alice, did you sleep well?" John asked.

"Yes, I did thank you, and you?"

"I slept like a log."

"Peter will arrive some time on Thursday. So he will be here in time for the party, and that makes the party doubly meaningful, doesn't it?"

"Yes, it does Norah," they both agreed.

"I take it that Brett has already gone?" enquired John, speaking to Norah, but looking at Alice.

"He's despicable," Alice muttered under her breath at the same time a little shiver ran down her spine. Norah didn't hear, or at least pretended not to hear what Alice had said. "Yes, he went out a bit before you came in," she answered.

"I'm making a brew; do you want one, John?"

"Yes, I'll have a cup of tea, please."

"Tea for you, too, isn't it, Alice, no sugar?"

"Yes, please, we'll take them into the workroom if that's ok with you, Norah." They settled down in the workroom to have a bit of free time together. Norah sensing this left them alone in peace. After about twenty minutes Alice looked at the clock.

"Good heavens, just look at the time. I've got to go, and get some work done. I'll have to go, John."

"I'll see you at lunch time, Alice, ok?"

At that Alice went out of the workroom taking with her the necessary things with which to do her cleaning, leaving John alone in the servants' workroom. He sat quietly at the table for a while deep in thought no sound came from the kitchen, or indeed from anywhere else. It was as if he was all alone in the house, for Alice and Norah had gone upstairs.

Eventually, after some time had elapsed, John picked up the cups that he and Alice had used and took them through to the kitchen on his way back to his office. John got rather busy and the next half hour or so went by rather quickly.

When the front door opened, and Brett entered the hall, he made his way to John's office. Pushing the door open, he stepped inside.

"Ha, John, did you make that appointment for me with my dentist?"

"Yes, I have made an appointment, for tomorrow at five pm."

"That's good. I suppose that you've heard that Peter is coming over, he will arrive probably sometime late evening on Thursday."

"Yes, Norah told me this morning, she was quite ecstatic about it, she's very fond of Peter," said John, grimacing acrimoniously.

"Are you all right, John?" asked Brett, rather taken aback by John's attitude towards him.

"Yes, I'm all right" he retorted, still rather abruptly.

"Whilst I'm here, have you received word from Lupton's confirming their order yet?"

"No, we have had no word from them as yet."

"Oh, I see, all right. Well, I'll be out for the rest of the day. Do you need anything before I go?"

"No, I'll be ok; I've got all I need."

"I'll see you tomorrow then." With that Brett left the office. He crossed the hall and went through the Dining Room. There was no one in; he entered the kitchen, the door to the workroom was open so he went inside, Norah was nowhere to be found. So after a few minutes, Brett left the house by the front door, closing it behind him.

Upstairs the two women were having a chat, about men in general and John and Brett in particular.

"John is so different, he's nothing at all like Brett," remarked Alice.

"Well, as you know, I have known Brett and Peter since they were boys and Brett was always the mischievous one, perhaps that's not the right word mischievous; more like, well, between you and me he could be spiteful. So the dirty trick he played on you came as no surprise to me really and that was not the first time he has done that kind of thing. He was seeing Margaret for quite a while."

"Let's not talk about him anymore, Norah, I hate him and only stayed on here because, well, the money is good, I do have to say in all fairness. That he increased my wages when I started going out with him, and he hasn't taken any money off me since then. Also because I live well within walking distance, you know what the bus service is like round here. If you don't drive it can be difficult getting to and from work in town, so I just put up with it, and stayed on in spite of everything."

As lunchtime approached, John pressed the full stop key on his typewriter and removed the envelope from the machine. He went through into the kitchen. There was no one in so he sat down at the kitchen table. He was deep in thought once more, and he buried his face in his hands. The situation he was in, he felt was hopeless. The secret that he had kept to himself for so long, and could end his new found love; he would have to reveal to Alice. He tried to convince himself that it would be better not to tell her yet. But subconsciously, he knew deep down that he was only kidding himself and that he would have to bite the bullet and tell her. The question was should he tell her right now, or would it be better to wait until they were completely alone this evening? He decided to wait; but was this because he just wanted to delay the inevitable?

His thoughts were interrupted by the very person that he needed to speak to. Alice came into the kitchen.

"Hi, John, my word you look deep in thought, penny for them."

"Hi, Alice, yes, I was deep in thought; I have something to tell you."

"What could that be that you have to tell me? That you still love me," Alice said, with her usual sweet smile.

"Yes, that, too, but I have something really important to tell you."

"Well, come on then, out with it."

"I can't tell you just yet, not here, Norah will be coming in very soon and I need to be alone with you. I'll come round tonight after work and tell you then."

The kitchen door opened and Norah came through and went over to the sink to wash her hands. "It's pouring down outside, what a change from all the sunshine we've been having lately, typically English weather."

"Yes", they all agreed with that.

Norah made a delicious lunch after which the afternoon passed rather quickly and uneventfully for all concerned, until five pm, the time that John and Alice finished work. John opened the car door for Alice and she got in. He drove up to her house.

"Well, it's stopped raining, anyway. What is it that you have to tell me that so important?" she asked.

"Let's get inside first, and then I'll tell you."

Once inside, John closed the door behind them, "Sit down please, Alice. What I have to tell you will probably come as a surprise or even a shock. I was really afraid of telling you in case you did not want to see me anymore. But I have to tell you now whilst our relationship is still new and hope for the best."

"So go on, tell me," Alice said impatiently.

"When I was born my mother, Mary died giving birth to me. She was only seventeen and unmarried. My father, James Peet, would have married my mother if she had lived. Of course, he never got the chance. Having a child out of wedlock back then, as I'm sure you know was taboo. So my mother had been abandoned by her family, when they found out that she was pregnant, and my father was only seventeen years old, too, and could not possibly bring me up on his own. So I was brought up by my grandparents, my father's parents, that is."

"Well, John, none of that is any fault of yours!"

"My mother was Nathan Northrop's twin sister and Nathan was Brett's father so that makes me Brett's cousin," John said, frowning.

"Oh my God, you're Brett's cousin! Well, you were right about one thing that certainly is a shock... I don't know what to say. I would never have guessed."

"This won't affect our relationship, will it, Alice?" John asked, nervously, awaiting her reply.

"John Peet, you are not Brett Northrop; you are nothing like him, not at all like him. And this revelation most definitely will not stop me from loving you." Alice sprang to her feet and threw her arms around him and she gave him the biggest kiss he'd ever had.

"Well, I wasn't expecting that," he said, flabbergasted. What was that for? Not that I'm complaining, of course."

"That was for being so frank with me, and telling me the truth."

"Does Brett know that you are his cousin?"

"I'm sure he does, but he has never broached the subject and obviously I've never said anything to him."

"Do you realize that if your mother had lived that you would have been a partner in the business?"

"Yes, I do know that."

"I wonder if that's the reason why he has never mentioned it to you. Or, if he does not know who you really are."

"Who knows? We may never know the truth, and I certainly won't approach him on the subject."

CHAPTER TEN
An Extract From The Dentist

Brett put his foot down hard on the accelerator of his car, the needle of the speedometer was bordering on seventy miles per hour. He was running late. It was twenty minutes to five and he was twelve miles away from Preston and his five pm appointment with Wil Cain, his dentist. It was two minutes to five as Brett grabbed his brief case from his car and dashed in through the door of the dentist's waiting room. There was only one other person waiting. He took a seat and waited his turn. Five or six minutes later, the previous patient came out of the surgery; followed by the beautiful young nurse carrying with her some dental records.

"Mr. Brett Northrop."

Brett got up from his seat,

"Come through, please."

Brett picked up his brief case and followed her into the surgery. "Sit down in the chair, please."

"Pass me his records, will you please, Joanne."

She handed Brett's records over to the dentist.

"It's just for a check up this time, isn't it, Joanne?" the dentist asked, as he explored the inside of Brett's mouth.

"Yes, just a check up, it's not six months since you were here last, Mr. Northrop," said Joanne.

"Well, I couldn't wait six months to see you again." Brett said in between the dentist probing his teeth.

"And I'll bet you say that to all the girls," said Jo, laughing.

To that, there was no answer forthcoming from Brett. The dentist completed his examination of Brett's teeth and concluded with: "Your teeth are in excellent condition, there is no work required this time."

Jo picked up the pile of record files from the worktop at the same time that Brett rose up from the chair. As Brett's shoulder collided with Joanne's elbow knocking the files from her hands and scattering them all over the floor. Simultaneously, his knee caught the glass of water sending that crashing to the floor as well, along with some instruments which were on the same stand.

In the pandemonium that followed the dentist was picking up his strewn instruments, some of which had gone under the base of the chair. Joanne was mopping up the water with some cloths, while Brett was picking up the scattered files and putting them back on top of the work unit.

"Oh, I'm awfully sorry, are you all right?" he asked Jo, putting his arm around her.

"Yes, I'm ok, thank you, you made me jump, that's all."

Brett fussed about with the files, straightening them up.

"Leave them, it's ok, I'll sort them out later," Jo said drily, as she ushered him out of the surgery, handing him his brief case as they went out through the waiting room where the last man still sat patiently waiting.

"We won't be a moment," Jo said, as she breezed past him on her way back into the surgery.

"I've never seen anything quite like that before," she said as she rummaged about amongst the mixed up files, hurriedly trying to find Mr. Kennedy's records. "Found it!" Opening the door, she stepped through into the waiting room. "Mr. Kennedy, sorry to keep you, please come through."

As Wil examined his patient, Joanne continued to sort out the rest of the files. The problem was that the contents had become completely mixed up as Brett had shoved everything into any file.

"Leave those now, Joanne and help me with this, please."

Jo took Mr Kennedy's notes from his file. Wil using his inspection mirror and probe checked his patient's teeth, "Upper left five."

"Upper left five," Jo repeated.

"I'm afraid this tooth will have to come out. Have you had Nitrous oxide before?"

"Yes, I have," replied Mr. Kennedy.

Jo checked his notes again. "Eighteen months ago; or you can have "painless" the needle. We would recommend the freezing for just one tooth," Joanne commented.

By the time that Wil had finished with his patient Jo had still not sorted out all the records.

"Leave them, Joanne until tomorrow, or you'll be here all night."

"Yes, I will," Jo agreed with that, so putting on her coat she said good night and left the practice, leaving Wil to lock up.

Meanwhile, Brett was on his way back home. He was not in the same mad hurry to get home as he had been to get to his appointment. As he drove, his thoughts ran back over the last fifteen or twenty minutes. Joanne probably thought that I was a complete idiot, but what must be, must be. He turned on the heater in the Jaguar to dry his trouser leg still wet from the water that splashed him when he had knocked over the glass.

After about five minutes, Brett was opening the car window, he was sweating what with the hot weather which had returned, and the car's heater on at full blast. But his trousers were dry by now, anyway. Ten minutes later, he was turning into the driveway at Northrop House. He parked his car and went into the house through the front door. Brett crossed the hall and entered his study closing and bolting the door behind him. He took the key to the safe from his pocket and opened it. Removing the contents from his brief case he deposited them into the safe, closing the door and after locking it, returned the key to his pocket. He went and sat down in his chair at his desk and threw his legs out at full stretch and leaned back. After a moment or two in this position, he leaned forward with his elbows on the desk and put his head in his hands. I'm glad today is over, Peter will be here tomorrow, he thought.

CHAPTER ELEVEN
Preparations

Thursday evening the 17th of July, nine fifty five pm; two days before the party. The door bell ringing brought Norah running to open it.

"Peter, oh, Peter," she threw her arms around him, "it's good to see you, I'll be bound."

"Norah Gray! Why you don't look a day older than when I last saw you, how are you?"

"Much better for seeing you, Peter, come in. Let me help you with your luggage. Is Brett with you?"

"Yes, he's right behind me, just parking the car up outside, he'll be coming in shortly."

Brett followed Peter into the house.

"Just look at you, two brothers together, well, I'll be bound. I'll go and put the kettle on."

"I'll have coffee, please, Norah, white one sugar," Peter said.

"Tea for you, Brett?" she asked.

Brett nodded.

"I'll go straight to bed when I've had my coffee; I've been travelling all day, I'm exhausted."

"Yes, I'm sure you are, Peter, Norah has got your old room ready for you."

"My old room, yes, I remember that."

They finished their drinks, and Peter related his journey from Canada. Then Peter went straight up to bed, and Brett went into his study, bolting the door behind him.

Friday morning 18th of July, the day before the party, the day got off to a flying start. By nine am everyone was busy. Brett and Peter were conversing in the Morning Room.

"Yes, the party that is scheduled for tomorrow was to be for the retirement of Bob Trafford, my works manager, but now, of course, it is also for your homecoming, too. I'm quite sure Bob won't mind that."

"I could do with getting some new shoes while I'm here, you know, a pair of brogues."

"Yes, we'll go to Manchester today and make a day of it, shall we, just like old times, hey! Peter."

John and Alice returned from the shopping trip which they had just made. It was just gone eleven thirty am. As they got out of John's car, Peter and Brett were about to leave.

"Hi you two, this is Peter," said Brett, "Peter, this is John Peet, my personal secretary and this is Alice. She's helping out with preparations for the party."

"Pleased to meet you," they both shook hands with Peter.

As Brett drove off with Peter, John and Alice unloaded the shopping from John's car and took it through into the kitchen. Norah and Alice set about preparing all the food that could be prepared, the day before the party. Norah was making cases for vol-au-vents, while Alice was busy shelling an abundance of peanuts. Conversation fluctuated between the brothers and the party.

"Like peas in a pod," Alice said her mind not really on what she was doing.

"John told me that there will be about fifteen people altogether at the party. Did you get the wine and the Champagne?"

"No, they will deliver that tomorrow."

"What have you ordered?"

As Norah spoke, John entered the kitchen.

"What wines have we ordered, John?"

"What wines? Let me see; he took a list from his pocket and read from it:

Chardonnay white 1952, one case

Chablis white 1955, one case

Beaujolais 1954, two cases

Champagne 1946,

Moet Shandon Brut imperial, two jeroboams."

"Well, that should do for starters," Norah interrupted giving a little chuckle. "I'm looking forward to a glass, or two, of Champagne."

"Especially while Brett's paying for it, too, hey, Norah," said John."

Alice nodded her head in agreement.

The traffic in Manchester was quite heavy as Brett and Peter entered the city centre. Brett parked the car outside of 'Ballantyne & White's' high quality shoes. They went inside and Peter tried on several pairs of shoes, finally settling for a pair of brown brogues.

"Well, Brett, shall we have some lunch? It's ten past one," said Peter.

"Yes, we'll go for some now." During lunch they were discussing the forthcoming party.

"I'll get something for Bob Trafford; does he smoke, Brett?"

"Yes, he smokes."

"Does he have a lighter?"

"I don't think so, he uses matches."

"I'll get him a cigarette lighter then, ok."

"My treat," Peter, said, as he paid the bill. "You're paying for the party and as that is also, in my honour, I'll pay for the lunch."

They left the restaurant and headed off down the High Street to look for a tobacconist shop. Across the road, Brett could see 'Edmondson's Gents' Hair Dressers'. Taking hold of Peter's arm he guided him to the edge of the curb. "Come on, Peter, look, Edmondson's, let us go and get a haircut.

"No," Peter said, "you go if you want to; I'll go and look for the tobacconists."

"Oh, come on, Peter, we used to go to Edmondson's when we were young. Let's go and have our hair cut together again."

"No."

"Oh, come on, it'll be like old times. Go on, for old time's sake."

"Oh, all right then, we'll go if it'll stop you pestering me."

They crossed the road and went into the barbers' shop and sat down. The interior of the barbers' had been refurbished since Brett had last been in. There were four new chairs, all of which were occupied. After about a ten minute wait, a chair became vacant.

"Go on, Peter, you go first."

Peter got up from his seat and went and sat in the chair. The door opened and an elderly gentleman came in and sat down next to Brett.

After some time had passed, it was Brett's turn to have his hair cut, whilst Peter was still not finished. Brett turned to the gentleman sat next to him. "It's all right, you can go, and I'll wait for this one," he said, indicating the chair that Peter was sat in.

A few minutes later, the barber finished cutting Peter's hair, and Brett went and sat down in the same chair, removing his glasses as he did so. Peter waited for Brett and after he had his trim they left the barbers' and went off once again in search of the tobacconists'.

"There it is!" said Peter after about a five minute walk. They crossed over the road and opening the door of 'The Silver Match Box' they went inside.

"I love the smell of tobacconist's shops," Brett said.

"We are looking for a cigarette lighter for a gift." The assistant brought out a display.

"Have you got something a little more expensive?" This time the assistant showed them a sample of gold plated lighters; from which Peter chose a particularly nice one.

"I'll take this one, please, could you gift wrap it for me?"

The assistant wrapped the cigarette lighter; they left the shop and spent the rest of the afternoon visiting more old haunts in Manchester that they used to go to when they were young, while Peter related in depth to Brett about the running of his lumber business back in Canada.

CHAPTER TWELVE
The Party

The day of the party had arrived at last. Norah and Alice were busy with just about everything that you could think of, that was necessary to make a running buffet successful. The dining table had been covered with a white linen tablecloth and all the food was covered over with paper or linen napkins. The Morning Room and the Living Room were also being prepared, and it was intended that the garden should also be used, weather permitting. The first guests to arrive at about six fifty pm were Bill Johnson with young Oliver and his mother, Margaret.

"Are we too early?" asked Margaret, as Norah opened the door.

"Not at all, come in, the other guests will be arriving soon. Frank's dad and Oliver will not be staying too late. Bill soon gets tired, we'll take Oliver and Bill home and Frank and I will come back later."

Margaret pushed Bill in his wheelchair into the Dining Room and settled him in a position convenient for him.

"What do you want to drink, Bill?" asked Norah.

"I'll have a whisky, please, Norah."

"Bell's, Teachers, Glen..."

"I'll have a drop of Teachers, if I may?"

"What can I get for you, Margaret?"

"I'll have a white wine, please."

"Do you want Chardonnay or Chablis?"

"I'll have Chardonnay, please."

"Do you want some lemonade, Oliver?"

Oliver nodded. Once again the door bell rang; Alice went to answer it. It was Dr. Hardman.

"Good evening, Doctor Hardman, come in." He followed Alice into the Dining Room.

"Good evening; everyone."

"Doctor Hardman! Is Elaine not with you?" asked Norah.

"No, she isn't, she's coming with your nephew, Anthony, I believe."

"Oh, is she now, and why am I not surprised to hear that."

"Can I leave my bag somewhere safe? I may get called out."

"Yes, you can leave it in the workroom, it will be safe in there," said Norah.

By seven thirty all the other guests had arrived. Brett was receiving the guests and introducing Peter to the ones who did not already know him. As promised, Anthony introduced Elaine to his Aunt Norah.

"Well, what do you think of her?" Anthony asked.

"She seems very sweet and first impressions are that she is quite intellectual, a nice girl."

"I knew you'd like her, Aunt Norah."

By now all the guests had dispersed themselves throughout the entire ground floor of the house and garden, with the exception of the office and the study. The doors to these were kept shut. The doors of the Living Room and the Morning Room were kept wide open to aid traffic flow as were the doors leading out into the garden. Brett was in the Living Room talking to Tom Laithwaite and his wife, Maureen. Both of them were stood with their backs to, and directly opposite the Morning Room door.

Brett was looking over Maureen's shoulder and drinking in Elaine Blake's entire being, who was standing sort of sideways on, but with her back to him, just inside the doorway of the room across the hall talking to Anthony.

"Don't look round, Elaine; but Brett is stood in the room across from us staring at you and his tongue is hanging out."

"His tongue is hanging out?" said Elaine.

"Well, you know what I mean," Anthony replied, "he's drooling over you."

"He's old enough to be my father."

"Phew, that won't matter to Brett. Anything in skirts is fair game to him."

"Well, I'm not," said Elaine indignantly, "he can look elsewhere." Elaine and Anthony moved away from the doorway and out of sight of Brett.

The party was going very well, everyone enjoying themselves to the full. Margaret, who was looking for Brett, found him in the garden talking to Sandra Kay. She had spoken earlier to Sandra's husband, Alan, whom she had seen talking to Tom and Maureen in the Living Room as she passed by the doorway. As she approached them she saw Brett pull himself away from Sandra. Although they were not alone in the garden, Brett did not seem to mind, until he saw Margaret coming towards them.

"Brett, when will the presentation take place? Bill is getting a bit tired," said Margaret, whilst ignoring Sandra completely.

"I'll find Peter," said Brett, looking at his watch, "and we'll do it now."

"He was talking to Norah and Dr Hardman in the Dining Room a few minutes ago. Shall I go and ask him to come and see you?"

"No, it's all right; I'm coming in a minute."

Brett went into the Dining Room and as he approached, Peter was telling Norah and Dr Hardman in some detail about the workings of his business in British Columbia in North West Canada.

"The men are called Loggers generally, but those who cut down the trees are called Fallers, they are cutting down trees some of which are over one hundred and fifty feet high. These are then put into holding pens to be later floated down the lake to the saw mill where the logs are cut up into all sizes from battens to beams."

"Peter! Can I interrupt you? It's time to make the presentation."

"Norah, will you make sure that everyone has got a glass of champagne, let me know when they have and I'll announce the presentation at about nine fifteen. In the meantime, Peter, we'll go and round up Bob Trafford and Tom Laithwaite."

Brett and Peter shepherded all the other guests, which were not already there, into the Morning Room where the presentation was to take place.

Alice and Norah went round giving everyone a glass of champagne while John Peet filled them up from the jeroboam for the forthcoming toast. At the allotted time Brett called them to order.

"Ladies and gentlemen, can I have your attention, please. As I'm sure you all know the party this evening, is a dual occasion. Initially it was to be in honour of the retirement of a long serving and respected member, of the staff of The Northrop Iron Foundry, Mr. Robert Trafford. But as I am sure that you are also well aware, it is also a welcome home to my brother, Peter whom I had not seen for some years. I am quite sure that Bob as he likes to be known, does not mind sharing the party with Peter. So as it is often said, without further ado; I hereby present Bob with what has become the traditional gift in retirement, from the company, this gold watch. I'm sure that I am speaking for all when I say that we wish you many happy years of joy in your retirement. Please raise your glasses to Bob."

At that everyone did indeed raise their glasses and gave a resounding cheer. Others also gave presents to Bob including Peter who gave him the gold plated cigarette lighter.

"May I also take this opportunity to welcome Tom Laithwaite, Bob's successor to his new position as Works` Manager." The applause died down. "Please enjoy the rest of the evening, eat and drink as much as you like and have fun."

After the presentation the guests soon spread out once more into little groups throughout the house and garden.

Margaret wheeled Bill who had nodded off after the presentation, out of the Morning Room and down the hall towards the front door. As she approached the bottom of the staircase opposite Brett's study door; she could hear voices coming from the other side of the stairs. It was Alan and Sandra Kay and they were arguing.

"Don't try to deny it;" said Alan, "how long has this been going on for? And I want the truth."

"There's nothing going on, Alan."

"Don't give me that, you scheming bitch, you're lying to me"

"I'm not lying to you, Alan. I wouldn`t do that."

"Huh! Yes, you are, I've suspected something's going on for some time."

"There isn't anything, honestly there isn't."

"You bloody little liar, I know there is!"

Margaret, who had stopped in her tracks when she heard the voices, smiling smugly, turned the wheelchair round and crept back along the hall to the Morning Room. As she entered John and Alice were just inside the doorway.

"Hello, Margaret, I thought you'd gone home," said Alice.

"Oh...I I've forgotten my key, I'll have to borrow Frank's."

"He's over there talking to Bob Trafford."

"Oh, yes, well, I'll see you when I get back." She went over to where her husband was and spoke to him. "Shall I take Oliver home with me, Frank, whilst I'm going?"

"Yes, you can do, he's in the Dinin' Room with Norah."

"I'll pick him up on my way through; I won't be long before I'm back." Margaret went into the Dining Room via the interconnecting door and taking Oliver with her, said to Norah that she would be back shortly. She did not leave by the Dining Room door which was almost opposite the front door as she could still be seen from the back of the staircase by Alan and Sandra. Instead, she went through the kitchen and out of the side door that led out to the footpath at the side of the house. She turned left and walked across the front of the house to her own front door.

Having settled Bill down comfortably for the night and putting Oliver to bed, she left her home through the back door and walked along the footpath at the southern end of the house. As she was passing by the open window of Brett's study she could see him sitting with his back to her at his desk. Margaret walked to the end of the footpath and went through the gate and into the garden. By now, twilight was falling, but it was still quite warm; she looked at the time by her watch, it was ten to ten and there were still people in the garden as she went up the steps and through the double doors into the hallway.

CHAPTER THIRTEEN
Suicide

"Could you draw the curtains for me, please, Elaine," asked Norah as she passed, carrying a large tray of food into the Living Room.

"Yes, I most certainly will," replied Elaine. She went over to the window and took hold of the curtains and pulled them across, as she did so one of the rings came unhooked from the top of the curtain.

"Oh, heck, look what I've done, Anthony."

"Awe, you've broken it," said Anthony, pulling her leg.

"Shut up and get me a chair to stand on, I can fix it, look there's one over there."

Anthony went over to the corner and brought the chair back to Elaine. She placed the chair against the window and slipped off her shoes. Taking hold of the chair back, Elaine put one foot on the seat and sprang up onto it. Standing on tiptoes she reached up and grasped the curtain ring of the heavy red velvet curtains with one hand. Anthony's eyes were glued to Elaine's exquisite legs, which somehow caused his ears to block up.

"Anthony...ANTHONY!"

"W...what?" stammered Anthony

"Help me down, please, it's done."

He held up his hand to help Elaine down from the chair.

"Thank you." She picked up the chair and put it back in the corner.

"You did that very well, Veronica," he said, teasing her.

"Yes, I did, Mark," Elaine replied, getting back at him.

Bob Trafford, his wife Annie, and Tom and Maureen Laithwaite, were in the Morning Room gathered round the radiogram. Maureen was looking through the large collection of records.

"What about this one? `April Love`, Pat Boone," asked Maureen.

"Yes put that one on," Annie agreed.

On hearing the strains of `April Love`, Elaine stepped across the hallway and entered the Morning Room. She had only been there about ten seconds when, who should come sidling up behind her but Brett. He slipped his arm around her waist. For a moment she did not move, and then she turned her head, seeing who it was and jumped back with her hand over her mouth. At the same time, Anthony entered the room and saw the whole thing.

"Oh my God, I...I thought it was you, Anthony."

Brett just stood there with a broad grin on his face.

"Sorry," he said, and backing away, he turned and walked out of the room.

Elaine had turned bright red and was visibly trembling.

"Brett!" muttered Anthony, "it's not your fault, Elaine; sometimes I could bloody kill him. Come and sit down for a minute. Will someone get her a brandy?"

"No, I'm ok, I'll be all right in a minute or so, I'm just a bit shaken, that's all."

Norah and Alice were by now back in the kitchen washing and drying glasses which they had collected from all over the house and garden.

"Norah!"It was Brett. "Peter has got a migraine; he has taken some pain killers and has gone up to his room for a lie down, he doesn't want to be disturbed for half an hour or so."

"Oh, the poor lad, I hope it doesn't spoil his day; that would be a shame."

As Brett left the kitchen; Alice agreed, "Yes, it would be a shame if it were to spoil his day. Does Peter get a lot of migraines?"

"Not that I am aware of."

A few minutes later, the hall clock struck ten thirty. Sometime after this John came into the kitchen looking for Alice.

"Alice! I've just been talking to Maureen Laithwaite and guess what she told me?"

"Go on, what did she tell you?"

"Earlier on this evening, Brett only tried it on with Elaine Blake. He crept up behind her and put his arm around her. Maureen said that Elaine was shaking like a leaf. And that Anthony was blazing mad."

"Well, that just goes to show what he's really like, doesn't it, and I'm not surprised. He's a womanizing fiend."

"John, do you know where the other jeroboam is?" Norah enquired.

"No, I don't know where it is, Brett has put it somewhere safe, I think."

"You don't know where he is, do you?"

"No, I've not seen him for a while."

"I'll go and look for him," and with that, Norah left Alice and John alone in the kitchen and went off in search of Brett.

Norah went into every room on the ground floor, in turn enquiring of guests the whereabouts of Brett. But no one had recently seen him. She approached Brett's study and knocked on the door. There was no reply. She knocked again a little louder, straining her ears above the noise of the party. Knocking on the door for a third time, she tried the door handle. To her surprise, the door did not open.

"Well, if it's locked he must be in there. "Brett!" she shouted as she knocked even louder. Still no reply was forthcoming from the study. Norah turned and walked back down the hall towards the kitchen where John and Alice were still talking.

"John, I've been knocking on Brett's study door and there's no answer, but he must be in there because the door is locked. Will you come and see if you can make him hear us."

At that John and Norah went back to Brett's study. First John tried the door handle; the door was indeed bolted on the inside. He knocked hard several times...No reply. John bent down and peered through the keyhole.

88

"Oh my God, he's collapsed, or had a heart attack. Go and fetch Dr. Hardman; Norah, quick!"

Norah hurried down the hall, although she was shaken by what John had said she still kept her head. The last time she saw the doctor he was in the Morning Room. Dashing through the door, she almost knocked Anthony over.

"Hey! Steady on."

"Oh, Anthony, thank God, where is Dr Hardman? Brett's collapsed with a heart attack or something."

"Heck! He's over here with Elaine." They threaded their way through the somewhat crowded room to where the doctor was sitting with his granddaughter.

"Come quickly, Doctor, Brett has collapsed in his study, he may have had a heart attack." said Norah, slightly out of breath.

Reaching the study, all four of them, Anthony and Elaine, followed by Norah and the doctor, found John still looking through the keyhole and shouting Brett's name.

"The door's bolted on the inside; we shall have to break in."

"Norah, will you fetch me my bag, please? It's in the workroom, I believe."

Norah went off to get the doctor's bag. Upon entering the kitchen she quickly related to Alice what had happened.

"I'll get the bag for you," said Alice dashing off into the workroom. She was back in a jiffy with the bag and the two women went and joined the men and Elaine at the study.

"Aunt Norah, will you and Alice make sure nobody comes up here while we sort this out, please."

"Yes, we'll do our best, come on, Alice."

"Stand back, I'll shoulder the door," said Anthony.

"Be careful, Anthony," said Elaine, thoughtfully.

"It's ok; I know what I'm doing." Holding down the handle, he stormed the door. The door creaked and sprang back but did not give way. Anthony charged at it once more and this time the door burst wide open. All four of them entered the room. Brett was sitting in his chair, slumped over his desk; his left shirt sleeve was pulled up past his elbow. On the desk to his right were a hypodermic syringe and an almost empty ampoule.

Doctor Hardman went up to the desk and took hold of Brett's wrist... "He's dead," he pronounced... "suicide, by all accounts."

Elaine frowned. "How long has he been dead?"

"I should say about half an hour, perhaps longer," said Doctor Hardman, who was still examining the body."

John stepped up for a closer look.

"Don't touch anything," said Anthony. "We'll have to call the police."

Doctor Hardman looked at the ampoule, but he did not need a second glance.

"Insulin, and he was not diabetic, if that ampoule was full it's no wonder he's dead."

"Oh, dear me, who's going to tell Peter," said John.

Elaine looked at her watch, it was twenty past eleven.

Anthony, excusing himself, squeezed past, between John and the bookcase to get behind the desk to the window. On examining it, he found it to be securely fastened.

"Well, no one came in through here, it`s locked."

"Will you go and get Aunt Norah for me, Elaine, please; I think she's the best one to let Peter know what's happened."

"Yes, I'll go and find her now, shall I, Anthony?"

"I suppose I had better go and ring the police."

"Will you, John; and Doctor Hardman stay with the body until I get back as we obviously can't lock the door."

"Can't you use this telephone?" asked John.

"No, its better not to touch anything until the police have been, even though it looks like suicide."

John nodded. "You can use the one in my office next door.

CHAPTER FOURTEEN
Anthony Takes Control

Anthony went into John Peet's cluttered office and picked up the telephone. He dialled the number of the local Police Station which he knew by heart. In his job he had contacted the local police many times. "Hello, Sergeant Rigby, its Anthony Hilton. I'm all right, thank you. I'm afraid that I have to report a suspected suicide... Yes, at Northrop House in Carr House Lane, Wrightington Bar, there's a party going on here... Yes, there will, I'll be here... Yes, all right, ok, I'll see you, then goodbye." He put down the telephone and went back to the study. "Sergeant Rigby will be coming round with an inspector as soon as he can get hold of one. There are obviously no detectives on duty at this time on a Saturday under normal circumstances, that is. Everyone must stay here until they arrive."

By now Elaine had found Norah and they went back to the study.

"Will you come with me, Elaine? I would rather someone else be there when I tell Peter that his brother is dead."

"Yes, of course, I will."

"Oh, poor Peter, he may be fast asleep, he went for a lie down with a bad headache, must be nearly an hour ago."

The two women crossed the hall and climbed the stairs. They turned right when they reached the landing and approached the second door.

92

"This is Peter's room." whispered Norah, as if she did not want to waken him."

Elaine knocked on the door and waited... she knocked a second time, after a few seconds the door slowly opened. She turned and looked at her companion, tears were streaming down Norah's face but not a sound was coming from her trembling lips. Elaine instinctively put her arm around her.

"Why, what's the matter, Norah?" asked Peter who was holding a compress to his forehead.

"Oh, Peter," she sobbed; throwing her arms around him. I've got some bad news for you, it`s B...Brett, he...he's committed suicide.

"Brett's, what...?"

"He's dead," Elaine added.

"No, he can't be, he was with me just before I came up here for a lie down. Where is he?"

"He's in his study; that's where he did it," Elaine said.

Whilst Elaine and Norah were breaking the bad news to Peter, Anthony had asked John to join Alice, to tell the guests what had happened and also that the unfortunate situation was that no one would be able to leave until the police had been. This left the doctor and Anthony on watch at the scene.

Peter, along with Norah and Elaine, came downstairs and crossed the hall to the study.

"Oh no, no, I had no idea! Why? He seemed perfectly normal, when I left him to go for a lie down. What on earth has made him do this?"

"Get him a stiff drink, will you, please, Elaine."

"Thank you, Anthony, I'll be all right."

"So your brother was perfectly ok when you left him, as far as you could tell?" asked Anthony.

"Yes, I don't understand what could have caused him to want to kill himself."

"Could he have had it in mind to do this for some time, do you think?"

"I don't know, as I have said; I had no idea that he had this in mind, or any reason, for killing himself."

"Would anyone like a cup of tea?" asked Norah.

"Yes, please, I'll have one if I may," Doctor Hardman said.

"Do you want a drink, Peter?"

"I'll have a coffee, please."

"Why not come into the kitchen where we can all have a sit down."

"You go for a brew," said Anthony, "I'll stay here; we can't leave the study unattended."

Elaine nodded. "I'll stay with Anthony." When the others had gone to the kitchen, leaving them quietly alone, he started to have a good look round. Reminding Elaine not to touch anything, he looked very closely at the syringe and the almost empty ampoule; the position of them? He next turned his attention to the door which, upon being forced by him had been flung wide open stopping about six inches short of hitting the front corner of the filing cabinet.

Looking at the bolt which was in its shot position with the tail turned up into the locked position, he could see that the two screws at the tail end of the bolt; that is the end nearest to the door hinges had been almost completely pulled out of the wood. On examining the door jamb, the receiver [staple] was completely missing, the screws having been pulled out from the door frame.

"Don't move, Elaine; can you see a small piece of polished brass with a couple of screws on the floor anywhere near your feet?"

She looked all around the floor close to her feet but there was no sign of the receiver.

"There it is, under the edge of the bookcase." Anthony squatted down to examine more closely the bolt`s receiver.

"Why are you so interested in that?"

"Well, can you see the two screws?"

"Yes, I can see the two screws, what about them?"

"The threads are full of compressed wood so that means that they were fully screwed into the wood when I forced open the door," he said, trying to impress her with his powers of deduction.

"Yes. What about it?"

"I was just making an observation, that's all."

"Well, I've made an observation, too," said Elaine.

"And what might that be, Sexton Blake?"

"Well, it might not mean anything, Mark Anthony," retorted Elaine, "it's just that the square bit of the bolt, that you get hold of is turned up and not down."

"So what does that tell you?"

"Well, nothing really, it just seems to me to be more natural to turn it down, that's all."

"Oh, I don't know that it matters."

"Mind you don't fall on your sword, that's all, Mark Anthony," Elaine said, with a mock smile.

"Ok, Vera."

"Don't you ever call me Vera, Ant, it`s Elaine, darling, to you," she said, this time with a genuine smile on her beautiful face.

"Elaine, darling," Anthony repeated.

John and Alice in the meantime had managed to gather all the guests together in the Morning Room and, whilst announcing the bad news about Brett's suicide, tried to keep everybody calm. The announcement of his untimely death, of course, had subdued the party atmosphere. And conversation now was all about the tragedy that had taken place that evening.

"What time did 'e die?" asked Frank Johnson.

"Well, as near as Doctor Hardman can tell, at the earliest, about quarter to eleven."

"I saw him at about ten minutes to ten through his study window, the curtains were undrawn and he was alive then," put in Margaret.

"Yes," Alice agreed. "I saw him in the kitchen just before ten thirty."

"How did he kill himself?" asked Tom.

"Well, it looks like he injected himself with a massive overdose of something."

Maureen frowned. "What of?"

"I can't tell you that," said John, glancing at Alice.

"The police may want to ask all of you or some of you at least, some questions, especially those of you who were the last to see him alive."

"'ow long will it be before they get 'ere?" asked Frank.

"I don't know for sure but they shouldn't be long now. Help yourselves to anything you like in the meantime. I'll let you all know when the police do arrive."

"Did he leave a suicide note or anything, an explanation of some kind" asked a tearful Sandra.

"Not that we are aware of, but of course there will have to be a full investigation when the police get here."

CHAPTER FIFTEEN
Inspector Grimshaw Investigates

At twelve thirty five am, Sergeant, Dick Rigby arrived with Detective Inspector, Tom Grimshaw. On hearing the front door bell Norah left the kitchen and opened the door to them.

"Good...ah morning Madam, I'm Sergeant Rigby, we received a phone call from here late on last night reporting a suicide."

"Yes, we did, or rather my nephew, Anthony Hilton reported it. Come in, please, I'll take you to the study that's where his body is, this way." Norah led the way to the study.

"The police are here, Anthony."

"Good morning, Sergeant Rigby," said Anthony; extending his hand in greeting.

"This is Detective Inspector Grimshaw."

"Hello."

"And this is Anthony Mark Hilton," said the sergeant, "he just happens to be a private investigator who was invited as a guest, to the party that was being held here last night."

"Well, I'm here now," said Inspector Grimshaw; "is this where the suicide took place?"

"Well, yes," said Anthony, "it is."

"And who found the body?"

"John Peet and Norah here were the first ones to realise that there was something wrong with Brett."

"There were four of us present when I broke the door open: John Peet, Doctor Hardman, who pronounced him dead, Elaine Blake, and me. John Peet has gone to let the other guests know what's happened, the doctor has gone to the kitchen for a brew."

"I shall need to speak to each of you; and anyone who saw him just before he died. But first things first, I must examine the scene where the suicide took place. Can you keep yourselves available, but out of the way?"

"We shall be in the kitchen if you want us." said Anthony and with that they all retired to the kitchen.

Detective Inspector Grimshaw looked first at the body and then at the syringe and the empty ampoule. "Insulin," then he looked at the broken bolt. He picked up the receiver from off the floor where Anthony had left it. "Well, they certainly had to break in; this has been forced from the door frame as you can see Dick."

"Yes, that's definitely been screwed fully into the woodwork as you say."

The inspector next went round the desk and viewed the body from behind. After a minute or two, he turned to face the window and drew back the curtains. "Well, the window is securely locked so no one came in or out this way," he said, grasping hold of and tugging at the locking mechanism.

Going back round the desk, he stood and looked all around the room. After a minute or so, his eyes rested on the oak cupboard with its double doors. Bending down, he grasped the handles of both doors and pulled hard at them. But they were locked.

"Someone could have hidden themselves in here and escaped after the study door had been broken in, if it had been left unlocked, that is."

Sergeant Dick Rigby who had been taking notes, whilst the inspector was checking things out said, "We haven't seen anything of a suicide note or anything of that sort yet, have we?"

"I'm just coming to that Sergeant. Give me a hand to lift the body off the desk and keep him in his chair, while I have a look in the drawers." After about ten minutes of searching through the desk, and the tallboy, the only items of furniture that were not locked, the search proved fruitless and no suicide note was to be found.

"Well, either it was a spontaneous decision or he wanted to keep the reason to himself. We'll have to search the body for keys to the filing cabinet, the cupboard, and the safe."

After searching through the pockets of the corpse, the only keys found were to his car and the filing cabinet. Brett's coat which was draped over the back of his chair proved to be void of keys or suicide note. Detective Inspector Grimshaw went over to the filing cabinet and inserted the key into the lock and turned it. He pulled open the top drawer. "There's nothing in here of any help at all." He looked through the other three drawers but all they contained were paperwork appertaining to the foundry.

"Well, I think that's all we can do in here for now at any rate there are no keys to either the cupboard or the safe."

"We'll interview the ones who broke in; and anyone else who saw him just before he died."

"I'll put some tape across the doorway," said Sergeant Rigby pulling the door closed as they left the study to go to the kitchen."

On reaching the kitchen the inspector found that the following people had been gathered there: [Not in chronological order]

Alice Bentham.

Elaine Veronica Blake.

Norah Gray.

Doctor John Hardman.

Anthony Mark Hilton.

Margaret Johnson.

Peter Northrop.

John Peet.

"I take it that these people are the ones that found the deceased's body or were the last known to see him alive, is that right?"

"Yes, that's right," replied Anthony handing him a scrap of paper.

"Let me see; so Mrs. Margaret Johnson you last saw the deceased at approximately ten minutes to ten through the then open study window is that right?"

"Yes, I had taken my father-in-law and my son, Oliver, home, and was on my way back via the footpath that goes past the study window."

"Are you sure that the window was open?"

"Yes, I'm positive; I could see the curtains moving with the breeze."

"Did he see you?"

"No, he was sitting in his chair at his desk with his back to me."

"And you are quite sure he was alive then?"

"Yes, quite sure," said Margaret."

"Now, Mr. Peter Northrop, the deceased's brother; at what time did you last see him alive?"

"I last saw Brett at around ten minutes past ten, I told him that I had got a bad headache, it could have been from the party, I don't know! He gave me some tablets, and I went up to my room to lie down. He said that he would see to it that I wasn't disturbed for half an hour or so and that is the last time that I saw Brett alive," said Peter, taking out his handkerchief and blowing his nose.

"Right then, next," said the Inspector. "Mr. Anthony Hilton and Miss Elaine Blake, you last saw him alive at about ten fifteen, in the Morning Room, is that correct?"

"Yes, that's correct," Anthony answered the inspector, "and we weren't the only ones."

"Twos enough for now," said Inspector Grimshaw, authoritatively.

"Now, it's the turn of..." he looked at the scrap of paper once more, "Miss Norah Gray and Miss Alice Bentham. What have you two got to say? At what time did you last see Brett Northrop alive?"

Norah took the lead. "Alice and I were washing glasses in the kitchen when Brett came in and told us that Peter had gone up to his room to lie down because of a migraine. That was just before ten thirty. We know that because the hall clock struck half past about a minute or two after Brett had left the kitchen; isn't that right, Alice?"

"Yes, that's right." Alice confirmed that it was as Norah had said.

"Well, now we come to the four people who broke into the dead man's study. They are, I believe:

Mr. Anthony Hilton,

Mr. John Peet,

Miss Elaine Blake,

Doctor John Hardman.

"Is that correct?"

"Yes, that is correct," said Anthony.

"At what time did you find the body?"

Anthony opened his mouth to speak but then...

Elaine interrupted, "It was precisely eleven twenty; I looked at my watch just as my granddad, Doctor Hardman, that is, was examining the body."

"I see, body found, twenty past eleven. Doctor Hardman at what time do you estimate the death to have taken place?"

"Well, I estimate the time of death to be no sooner than ten forty five, perhaps later."

"On what do you base the estimated time of death?"

"Taking into account the ambient temperature and the warmth of the body and of course, my past experience, I think that my estimation is fairly accurate."

Death by suicide at approximately ten forty five pm, on the 19th July 1958, wrote Detective Inspector Tom Grimshaw.

"An open and shut case, if ever I saw one. There may, of course, have to be a Coroner's inquest, but I'm sure it would just be a formality. Someone will come round for the body in the morning and may also wish to see someone just to clarify a few things. For instance we have found no note from the deceased and no keys to either the big cupboard or the safe. So there is just one more thing to do, can his next of kin identify the dead man?"

"Yes," said Peter. "I'm clearly his brother; I can identify him as Brett Northrop."

CHAPTER SIXTEEN
Sexton Blake

After the departure of Inspector Grimshaw and Sergeant Rigby the guests started to leave. Peter thanked them all for coming and the people all gave him their condolences. Some of course, were just out of politeness and some were genuinely sincere.

"Aunt Norah," said Anthony, putting his arm around her, "Elaine and me will come back in the morning before they come for Brett's body so we can help out and to support you and Peter, of course."

"Yes, thank you, I would appreciate that Anthony, and you too, Elaine, thank you love, you're a good girl." As Norah said these words tears began to flow down her cheeks. Elaine put her arms around her and hugged her.

"Will you be all right?" she asked.

Norah nodded her head, whilst at the same time trying to dry her eyes with her hankie. When the last of the guests had gone, Elaine and Anthony said goodnight to Norah and to Peter and left a saddened Northrop House.

"I am going to go upstairs to bed now, Norah; I'll see you in the morning, goodnight."

"Good night, Peter, oh, I am so sorry you've only been here two days and you've lost your brother."

"I know Norah, it's been a big shock, I don't know why he has done such a thing as committing suicide. He seemed to be perfectly normal with nothing bothering him. I just don't understand it at all."

Peter climbed the stairs and went up to his room.

Norah was left alone with her thoughts, she went to the kitchen, there were still lots of food left over and although she and the girls, namely: Alice, Elaine and Margaret had made use of the time that they had while the inspector was in the study investigating the death of Brett, to get a lot of pots and glasses etc washed and put away, she still felt that there was a burden of work to be done.

"Thank God, that Elaine and Anthony are coming back in the morning; I don't know what I'd do without them. Tomorrow, well, it's today now, it is Sunday and John would not normally be here either. I suppose I had better go up now and try to get some sleep." So with the two brothers on her mind, Norah went upstairs to bed with a heavy heart, and cried herself to sleep.

It was early Sunday morning and although he'd not had much sleep, Anthony called round at No.91 Pepper Lane where Elaine lived with her parents and they set off to go back to Northrop House. "I'm surprised that you were waiting for me, I honestly thought that you would be still in bed," said Anthony.

"Oh, I wish I was, I've not woken up yet," said Elaine putting her hand over her mouth while yawning.

Anthony's car hit a pothole in the road, "Now, you've woke me up again," said Elaine, "and I was just getting back to sleep."

"Never mind, we'll soon be there, I'm sure my Aunt Norah will make you a coffee and that will wake you up."

At twenty minutes to nine, Anthony's car turned into the drive at Northrop. As he pulled up in front of the house, Norah came to the door. "Thank you for coming both of you," she said, as she threw her arms around Elaine and gave her a big hug. "Come in, they have just rang to say that someone will come for Brett's body at half past nine."

"How is Peter?" asked Elaine

"He's still in bed, I've let him sleep, it will do him good."

"How sad that he should lose his brother in that way and he's only been over here two days."

"Yes, it's sad. Come in, would you like a drink?"

"Oh, yes, please, I'll have a coffee."

"What do you want to drink, Anthony?"

"I'll have coffee, too, please, Aunt Norah."

They all went through into Norah's sitting room and sat down to have their drinks.

Anthony got up. "I'm going to have a look in the study, if you don't mind, that is, Aunt Norah, before they come for Brett. I just want to have a final look round, if that's ok with you?" "Yes, you go and pay your last respects if you want to, I can't find it in me, to come with you."

"Can I come, too?" asked Elaine.

107

"I suppose so, come on." On reaching the study door they found that it had police tape across it.

"We'll have to remove some of this and put it back after," said Anthony.

They pulled away sufficient tape to allow them to get through the door and entered the room. Anthony crossed over to the far wall and pulled back the curtains, as the daylight flooded the small room they could clearly see that Brett's body had been laid out on the floor in front of the bookcase.

"Sergeant Rigby and Inspector Grimshaw will have laid him out here, because of rigor mortis they could not leave him in his chair over night."

Anthony looked all around the room. Brett's coat was still draped over the back of his chair. He put his hand into one of the pockets and took out Brett's gold cigarette lighter; he felt in the other one and pulled out a folded white monogrammed handkerchief with the intertwined letters 'BN' embroidered in one corner.

"What are you looking for?" asked a curious Elaine.

"I don't know; anything, perhaps a suicide note or something that might tell us why he killed himself."

Elaine picked up Brett's glasses from the desk, where someone, probably the inspector had left them. She turned and looked at Brett's body.

"He looks just like Peter without his glasses on, doesn't he?" she said.

"Yes, you can tell that they were brothers all right, and he had a spare pair of glasses in the top pocket of his coat." Anthony felt inside the coat and pulled out an expensive looking leather wallet which also had the same 'BN' monogram embossed on it; also his leather bound cigarette case. He opened the wallet and looked inside. "There's nearly fifty pounds here, and receipts and other stuff, but nothing to say why he killed himself."

Elaine had by now gone over to the door and was looking once more at the bolt. It still didn't make any sense to her why the tail of the bolt was turned up. She took hold of it and slid it backwards and forwards, turning the tail alternatively up and then down, this convinced her that she was right, it was easier to turn it down. Then she noticed a small fragment of some kind of fibre fast on the upper corner of the bolt just where the tail goes to engage in the unlocked position.

"I'm just going to get my handbag, Anthony." She left the study and went back to the Sitting Room and came back with her handbag. Elaine opened her bag and took from it a manicure set. Opening it, she took out a pair of tweezers and picked the small piece of fibre off the bolt, and placed it carefully inside the manicure set, replaced the tweezers and closing the lid, she put the manicure set back into her handbag.

"There's nothing here to tell us anything," said Anthony, "we may as well go."

They left the study and closing the door, they replaced the police tape across the doorway.

As they entered the kitchen, the hall clock struck nine thirty.

Norah was just washing up the cups which they had used.

Ten minutes later, a black van arrived. Norah opened the door to find an elderly grey-haired man with a rugged stone-like face, and a tall thin gentleman with horn-rimmed spectacles, both dressed in black suits with black ties.

"Good morning, we're from the Coroner's office," the bespectacled man croaked in a low voice. "We've come for the body of hmm..." he held up a clipboard. "A Mr. Brett Northrop, I believe."

"Yes, come along inside, my nephew will show you where the body is."

The two men followed Norah into the kitchen and she introduced them to Elaine and Anthony who took them both to the study.

As they approached the door, Peter was just reaching the bottom of the stairs. He saw the men. His face changed to ashen, "My poor brother." He wiped his eyes on his handkerchief, "to lose him so soon, and after not seeing him for so long."

"He's in here I take it?" The stone-faced man asked.

"Come on, Peter," Elaine said, putting her arm around him, "come with me, Norah will make you a drink."

While Elaine took Peter to the kitchen, Anthony showed the two men into the study; where they proceeded to remove all the items from Brett's clothes and placed them into a brown paper bag. "Will you sign here, please?" croaked the tall thin man; offering the clipboard to Anthony.

Within half an hour the men from the Coroner's Office had left, with Brett's body in the black van.

"Where have they taken him?" asked Elaine in a low voice.

"To the mortuary at Wigan Infirmary," Anthony replied equally softly so as not to upset Peter. "For the time being at least as it's Sunday."

"The tea's brewed," Norah announced.

"That'll be lovely," said Peter.

"Nothing beats a cup of tea, supposed to cure all ills," Elaine smiled brightly. "Oh, I'd forgotten, you like coffee, don't you?"

"That's all right, Norah," remarked Peter sombrely. "I'll have tea. When in England, do as the English do."

"Oh, while you're here, Anthony, I'll give you a key for the front door then you can let yourself in if you need to for anything, if that's all right with you, Peter?"

"Yes, of course, it's all right, Norah."

"Thank you, I'll let you have it back when all this trouble blows over."

CHAPTER SEVENTEEN
Liaison

Alan Kay stared at the letters in his hand. His knuckles turned white and his Adam's Apple jumped as he swallowed hard.

"What are you looking at?" asked Sandra, inquisitively.

"You...you... you've definitely been having an affair! And these letters are the proof."

"What letters?"

"As if you didn't know! The letters sent to you, from that swine, Brett."

"He's dead. It's not right to talk like that about someone who's dead."

"He was a swine. And I'll say what I like about him."

"And you've been nosing around in my things, haven't you?"

"What if I have? You've been carrying on with someone else. I've never looked at another woman since I met you."

"No good in the bedroom, though, are you?"

"How dare you, I could bloody well kill you!"

"You wouldn't dare. You couldn't kill a flipping fly."

He lashed out, `SMACK!!`

Sandra squealed and rubbed her cheek. "You're a wife-beater that's what you are! And give me those letters, they're private."

At this, he threw them at her. They lay on the floor accusingly; scooping them up she ran out of the room, crying.

Sandra lay on her bed, the sodden letters beside her. She`d loved Brett so much. She`d be glad when the inquest, and his funeral were over.

Her thoughts turned to their first liaison.

She`d been leaving her office to catch a bus home as Alan would be working late for the next few nights, when she recognised Brett's car. He opened the door. "Would you like a lift?" he asked, smiling at her.

A spot of rain touched her cheek. She`d be soaked through if she waited for the bus. "All right then, that`s good of you."

She got into the car and settled herself beside him. Within minutes, she was home. "Will you come in for a cup of tea?"

He shook his head. "I`ve got an appointment."

The following evening he was waiting outside her office again. "Lift?" he asked.

She climbed in.

"How about us going for a drink before I drop you off?"

She bit her lip. "I don`t think I should. Alan wouldn't like it."

"We won`t be long," he said, wheedling. "I know you`ve been working hard. A drink will help you unwind."

"We have been very busy, I must admit. Oh, all right then."

His eyes gleamed. "Good!"

They drove to a country pub `The Hay Rick`. It had a thatched roof and roses round the door. He helped her out of the car. "A gentleman, I see," she quipped.

They entered the pub. A pitchfork adorned one of the walls, and the others had prints in dark frames of oldie worldly country scenes.

"What will you have to drink?" he asked.

"Port-and-lemon, please," she replied, as she seated herself at one of the circular well-polished wooden tables, while he went up to the bar.

He returned with a whisky and soda for himself; and a port-and-lemon for her.

She took a satisfying sip of her drink, and looked around taking in the ambience of their surroundings. "This is nice."

He smiled with satisfaction. "I'm glad you like it. I often come here."

"On your own, I hope?"

"Of course, on my own, you know you're the only girl for me."

She giggled "You say so."

They chatted for a while.

With a soulful look, he suddenly burst out. "Alan's a lucky dog to have you."

She giggled again and blushed. "Do you really think so?"

He reached out and touched her hand. "I do. If only I had met you first."

She removed her hand from beneath his. "I'd best go."

"Must you?"

"Yes, I'd better," she said reluctantly.

He drove her home.

She wasn't surprised that he was waiting for her the following evening. In fact, she had been watching the clock in anticipation of his being there. This time, on their way to her house, he took a detour down a narrow country lane. "A short cut," he explained.

He stopped the car and turned to her. How it happened, she'd never know, but suddenly emotion bubbled up inside her, and their lips met in a long lingering kiss. He pulled away. "I shouldn't have done that," he apologised.

"It was as much my fault as yours," she murmured.

"Oh, no, the fault's all mine." Their lips met again, and again.

She felt his hand on her knee. His fingers moved up her leg and he began toying with her suspender. Of course, she couldn't resist. In a few moments, her skirt was around her waist, her blouse buttons undone, and the car was rocking on its suspension, with the windows steamed up.

A door banged bringing her back to the present. She sighed. Alan's still in a bad mood! Will he ever get over it? After all, Brett is dead, she pondered; a tear rolled down her cheek. Why, why, had Brett taken his own life? She had loved him so much, and she knew that he had loved her. What on earth could have driven him to do such a thing? Was he being blackmailed, was it a problem with

115

his business? Try as she may she could not come up with any logical conclusion.

CHAPTER EIGHTEEN
The Inquest

The day of the inquest arrived at last, much to Sandra's relief.

It was to be held in Wigan. Peter looked around the courtroom.

The Coroner, Mr. William Thompson, who had a sharp nose and red thread veins running over his sallow cheeks was seated at the bench, and in front of him were the interested parties.

The Coroner, having made a few relevant remarks about the terrible nature of the tragedy which they had come to investigate that morning, outlined the case. Witnesses would be brought forward to identify the deceased as Brett Northrop, the owner of Northrop House, where he had been found dead in a room which was locked from the inside by a bolt.

It would be shown that no other way into or out of that room was possible, as the only other way, was through a window which was also locked from the inside.

Dr. Hardman gave his evidence as to the time and cause of death.

Other witnesses told of how Brett had been that evening, and how they knew of no reason why he would want to kill himself, as he had behaved quite normally, and seemed to be his usual self.

After lunch; the remaining witnesses gave their evidence and the coroner summed up as follows:

"On hearing all the evidence of this sad case: the room, Brett Northrop's own study, the door of this was bolted on the inside, with no other way in or out. The syringe, the almost empty insulin ampoule; the number of people present when the door was forced open, and all other statements of facts being taken into account; I can only conclude that, on Saturday the 19th July 1958, Mr. Brett Northrop committed suicide whilst the balance of his mind was disturbed, and that is the verdict of this inquest."

Sandra could contain herself no longer, she broke down crying, dabbing her eyes with her handkerchief and sobbing, "Brett, Brett." The scalding tears ran down her pale cheeks falling onto her dress forming dark spots on the light-coloured fabric.

"Pull yourself together," muttered Alan as they left the hearing, "you're showing yourself up."

As they reached the car, he opened the passenger door. "Get in!" he snarled. He pushed her roughly into the car, slamming the door.

"Ouch! You've no need to be so horrible."

"What do you expect; you crying in public over another man; making a fool of me?"

"I'm sorry. I couldn't help it."

He started the engine. "Is it any wonder I'm angry with you, you bloody tart, carrying on with Brett the way you did?"

As he drove off, not really concentrating on his driving, a small van came out of a side road, Alan swerved and braked hard just missing the side of the van. "Now look what you've made me do, a bloody woman driver, I might have known, it's all your fault. From then on for the rest of the journey, a grim silence fell over them.

Outside the building, Norah turned to Alice. "Are you and John coming back to Northrop for a brew?"

"I'll ask John." She turned, smiling sweetly. "Can we call at Northrop House on the way back?"

"Of course, we can, Alice."

They drove the twenty minute journey back to Northrop House.

In the kitchen, Norah kicked off her shoes. "Oh, they're killing me."

"That's a good idea, these brogues are a bit tight, it's the newness," Peter remarked.

"Put the kettle on, Elaine, will you?"

When it had boiled, Norah made the drinks. They sipped at them.

Norah gathered up the tea cups when they had all finished and put them in the sink. "Come on, girls, let's go into my parlour and leave the boys on their own for a bit."

"What do you think of Sandra, Elaine? She was sobbing her heart out. Alan's face was like thunder."

"Yes, I noticed that," broke in Alice.

Elaine shivered, "I'm glad I'm not Sandra, I wouldn't want to be in her shoes."

"No, me, neither," murmured Alice.

"Peter what will happen to Alice and Norah too, for that matter, will they both be kept on here?"

119

"Don't worry yourself about that, John; things will carry on just as before. I will be staying on here for a while myself to see to the business as I'm now the sole owner of the iron foundry. I will, of course, eventually have to go back to Canada and probably leave the foundry in the hands of Tom Laithwaite, Alan Kay, and yourself, of course. But for now; let's get the funeral over and I'll sort something more permanent out, ok."

"Yes, thank you, Peter, I know that Alice and Norah will be relieved to hear that and me too, for that matter. I'll tell them, to put their minds at rest."

The following morning, Peter and John drove to the Registrar's office to collect the death certificate.

"Shall we go to the Undertakers now, while we're out, John?"

"Yes, we may as well. Walsh's at Standish? They do a good job." John directed Peter as he drove to Standish. They pulled up outside of Walsh's funerals. John and Peter entered the gloomy parlour. Through a purple curtain in one corner of the room emerged a sullen grey-haired man. "Good morning, gentlemen, can I be of assistance to you?"

"Good morning, I would like to arrange a funeral, please for my brother."

"Your brother; yes, certainly sir, what is the name of the deceased?"

"Brett Northrop."

"And do you have a death certificate, or do you want us to do that for you?"

"Yes, we have just come from the Registrar's office," replied Peter, handing over the death certificate.

"Do you want to make the arrangements now?"

"What do you think, Peter, do you want to do it now?" asked John.

"Yes; why not."

"Is the deceased to be cremated or buried?"

"Hmm, well, I'm afraid his death was suicide," remarked John.

"Oh, yes, I see," the undertaker said, as he looked at the death certificate.

"Brett would have wanted to be cremated, anyway," commented Peter.

"Yes, I suppose he would, I seem to remember him saying that once."

"So it's to be a cremation then, at Wigan? By the way, my name's Stanley Melling, he put out his hand. We can offer you a range of coffins that we use for cremations."

"We want a good quality one!" Peter exclaimed.

"All our coffins are of good quality, Mr. Northrop. If you will please step this way into the back room you can choose one of them."

Peter chose a nice rosewood coffin, no expense would be spared.

"Where is the deceased at the moment? I shall have to measure him, of course, and would you like us to bring him back here to the Chapel of Rest?"

"Yes, please, I was just about to ask you about that, at the moment he's at the mortuary in Wigan."

"I'll arrange to have him brought here; and may I offer you my sincerest condolences in your bereavement."

At these words Peter took out his handkerchief wiped his eyes and blew his nose.

"How about flowers; shall I arrange a florist for you?"

"Yes, please. And will you put an obituary in the Observer, too?"

"Certainly, Mr Northrop, we will see to all that for you."

CHAPTER NINETEEN
The Funeral

The funeral was arranged for the 4th of August. It was a wet day which seemed to match the mood of the mourners who were huddled under umbrellas as the hearse containing the body of Brett Northrop drove into the grounds of the crematorium. The coffin with the wreath of Brett's brother, Peter on top of it, was carried into the building by Peter, John Peet, Anthony, and Tom Laithwaite. The other wreaths and sprays were left inside the hearse.

The mourners, all dressed in black, most of them female, some of whom were wearing black hats with black veils over their faces in an attempt to hide their distress, were sobbing into handkerchiefs

Sandra raised her face and blew her nose loudly. She glared at these females. There were so many of them. Who were they? She recognised Alice Bentham and Margaret Johnson, but the majority she didn't know. Were they all, former lovers of Brett? She clenched her fists and dug her nails into the palms of her hands. They had no right to be here, she alone was the one he really loved! Her stomach churned and she felt like choking the life out of these other women – bitches, the lot of them!

Sandra was so upset she hardly heard the words of the Eulogy given by Peter, followed by Tom

Laithwaite praising what a good employer Brett had been and how he would be much missed.

At that moment, the organ struck up:

ABIDE WITH ME
1
Abide with me fast falls the eventide
The darkness deepens Lord with me abide
When other helpers fail and comforts flee
Help of the helpless o abide with me
6
I need thy presence every passing hour
What but thy grace can foil the tempters power?
Who like thy self, my guide and stay can be?
Through cloud and sunshine Lord abide with me
7
I fear no foe, with thee at hand to bless;
Ill's have no weight, and tears no bitterness.
Where is death's sting? Where grave thy victory?
I triumph still, if thou abide with me.

After this, there were a couple of prayers led by the vicar of Saints, Peter & Paul. She choked on the words of The Lords Prayer 'Our Father...'

Alan seated beside her glared and hissed. "I'm fed up with this, you're showing me up again. Pull yourself together!"

"I can't help it," sniffed Sandra.

"You'd better help it or I'll see my solicitor about a divorce – and you can sling your hook!"

"But, Alan, where would I go?"

"Who cares, you can go to hell with Brett, as long as I don't have to hear you caterwauling all the time. I hope he gets a good roasting, if anyone deserves it, he does."

Sandra looked shocked. "Don't be so callous."

"I'll be what I like."

At last the service was over and the purple velvet curtains slowly drew together, Brett's coffin disappearing from view.

Alan heaved a sigh of relief as the mourners followed each other out of the building and piled into the cars to be taken to the Scarisbrick Hotel at Wrightington Bar to partake of the funeral meal.

Elaine put her knife and fork down. "I was talking to my uncle last night, Anthony. I was telling him about Brett's suicide, and he told me something that quite frankly shook me."

Anthony swallowed his last mouthful of food. "Oh, what did he say?"

"He said that when he was young, a friend of his had shown him a trick. This friend had put him into a toilet cubical and bolted the door from the outside using a piece of thin string. He said it was done so quickly and easily he could hardly believe what he had seen. I asked him exactly how it was done and he said that his friend lined up the bolt so that it would slide shut, and he then took the string and put the two ends together, and looped the other end onto the bolt handle. As he closed the door he took the two ends of the string round the edge of the door to the outside, and jerked the string. The bolt shot across and he immediately jerked the string downwards turning the bolt into the locked position.

He then let go of one end of the string and pulled the other end until the string came out of the door."

Anthony looked thoughtful. "Well, you surely don't think that's what happened in Brett's case, do you?"

"Do you remember me saying that it did not seem right that the tail of the bolt was turned up," Elaine remarked.

"Yes."

"What I didn't tell you was that I had found some sort of fibre stuck on the bolt as well, which I kept in my manicure case."

"Do you still have it?"

"Yes, I've still got it."

"You know, if this theory of yours is correct then it means that someone may have murdered Brett."

"Yes, it would, wouldn't it? So, Anthony, are we going to try this theory out?"

"Mmm... I was just thinking we could use the bathroom at Northrop House, that door has a similar bolt on it. We don't want to use Brett's study for two reasons. First, the bolt would have to be re-fixed to the door, also we don't want to draw attention to ourselves and upset Norah, or Peter, do we?"

"No, that's true," agreed Elaine.

"Well, then we'll go back to Northrop House on Thursday. And if we can, we'll try this idea of yours out and see if it really does work."

"What time will you pick me up, Anthony?"

"About one o'clock, will that be ok?"

"Yes, and bring some fine cord or thin string with you."

On the afternoon of Thursday 7th August, Elaine was waiting for Anthony as he drew up in his car.

"Have you brought the string with you?" she asked as she got in beside him.

"Yes," Anthony replied as he drove off. "And as Aunt Norah will have gone to see my mother, we only have to make sure that Peter or John does not see us doing this."

"Good, we don't want any awkward questions, do we?"

"No, certainly not, this is only a theory, and even if it works it does not prove that Brett was murdered. What about motive and opportunity?"

"What about motive, you say?" croaked Elaine, "I for one know of someone who said, 'Sometimes, I could b...well kill Brett' and a room full of people heard him say it."

"Why, you don't think I killed him, do you? Sometimes one says things on the spur of the moment, out of anger or frustration, but that does not mean they would do it."

"No, I agree, but you said, what about motive? I think you'll find quite a few people who wouldn't mind seeing Brett Northrop dead, perhaps Alan Kay to name but one."

"Yes, well, you could be right, and certainly all who were at the party had opportunity."

CHAPTER TWENTY
Tied Up With String

The car turned into the driveway and Anthony pulled up outside Northrop House.

"Oh," said Elaine "there's no car here; Peter must be out, so we've only got John to worry about."

"We'll go in and I'll tell John that we've come to pick up something for Aunt Norah."

"That's a good idea."

Anthony took the latchkey from his pocket and opened the door; they went inside and stood quietly listening for a few moments, there was no sound coming from within.

"We'll go to John's office and see if he is in there."

"There's no one in, it looks like there's no one here."

"That's a stroke of good fortune then, isn't it?"

"Let's go to the bathroom then."

As they reached the bathroom, Elaine said, "You do it, Anthony."

"No, it's your idea, you do it."

"No," insisted Elaine, "I'll go in the bathroom."

"All right then, I'll do it."

Anthony was just about to loop the string on to the bolt when they heard the front door open, and footsteps going down the hall. Anthony darted into the bathroom pushing Elaine in front of him.

"We can't stay here, whoever that is will have seen your car," whispered Elaine.

"Yes, I know, you sneak out and go through the kitchen into Aunt Norah's workroom and wait there for me. Meanwhile I'll go and see who it is, and give them some excuse for being here."

"All right" answered Elaine, while keeping her voice down to a whisper.

Anthony opened the door a few inches and peered through. "It's ok, the coast is clear, off you go."

She removed her shoes and darted down the hall and disappeared into the Dining Room, leading to the kitchen.

Anthony, meanwhile went down the hall and turned the corner.

"Hello, Anthony" It was John Peet. "I thought you were here, I saw your car outside."

"Hello, John, I've just called in to pick up Aunt Norah's purse for her."

"I can't stay, I'm afraid, Anthony, I've only come to pick up some paperwork; Lupton's have confirmed their order for quite a large casting. They are good payers so we have to look after them."

Five minutes later, John had gone; leaving Anthony and Elaine alone once more.

Back at the bathroom they were once again attempting to lock the door with the string.

"Come on, Ant, you're trembling like a leaf."

"It's all these interruptions making me nervous."

Anthony's trembling hand slipped the loop of string over the end of the bolt, he lined the bolt centrally so it could slide taking the ends of the string round the edge of the door, he closed it gently.

"Are you ready?" he shouted through the closed door.

"Yes, hurry up and don't forget to jerk the string upwards as well."

Anthony gave the string an almighty jerk, and then jerked it upwards. "Has it worked?" he shouted to Elaine.

She opened the door. "Well, the bolt shot all right but the tail did not engage in the locked position, it didn't move the tail far enough."

"I pulled the string hard in both directions."

"Well, I don't know why it didn't work properly," admitted Elaine.

"Let's try again," she said... "Just a minute something's just occurred to me. Let's go to the study."

"You know we can't try it there."

"I don't want to try it; I just want to look at the door, that's all."

"What good will that do?"

"I don't know yet if I'm right I'll tell you, if I'm wrong I won't." She said, with a cheeky grin on her pretty face.

They entered the study, Elaine carefully examined the door.

The bolt was still hanging on, just as it was the night that Anthony had to break in.

"Well, that's good, I wondered if Frank Johnson may have removed it as it was Brett who wanted the bolt put on in the first place."

Elaine was hardly listening to him; she was deep in thought..."Mmm...Come on back to the bathroom, Anthony."

"What's all the mystery then? What does all this mean?"

"You're supposed to be the detective, you tell me."

Anthony shrugged his shoulders, "Search me, I haven't a clue."

"Well, if I'm right, you'll know."

They made their way back to the bathroom once more.

"Right, Ant, try it again, but this time jerk the string downwards."

Elaine went into the bathroom and Anthony looped the string onto the bolt, taking the ends around the door edge, he closed the door. He jerked the string outwards and downwards.

"Has it worked?"

Elaine opened the door; a huge grin on her face, "It worked perfectly and do you know why?"

"No, to be honest, I can't see what difference it makes."

"Well, if you look at the bolt in relation to the latch, which is operated by the handle, you can see that on this door the bolt is below the latch. Whilst on the study door the bolt has been put on above the latch. So when we first tried to bolt the door the latch stopped the string from going far enough to turn the tail of the bolt up into the locked position."

"Yes, I can see what you mean, so in the case of the study door it's the opposite effect, you could not turn the tail as you call it down because the latch would get in the way and stop the downward movement of the string."

"And that's why the tail was turned up," remarked a triumphant Elaine.

"Right, Elaine, so are you satisfied? Or do you need to do it again?"

"No, we don't need to do it anymore if you're happy with it, Anthony."

"Have you got your manicure set with you?"

"Yes, why?"

"Let's have a look at that fibre?"

She took the manicure set from her bag and carefully opened it.

"Oh, no," she gasped, "it's gone!"

"It's what?"

"It isn't here," she said as she hurriedly removed one instrument after another.

"Oh, it's here, under the nail file, thank God."

"I thought for one minute you'd blown it, Sexton."

"Well, I haven't, Ant, see." She held up the tweezers; holding a red fibre about half an inch long in the jaws.

"Let's have a closer look at it." He took it from her and studied it closely. "Do you know, Elaine, the carpet in Brett's study could be the same colour as this. Let's say for instance that Frank Johnson dropped the bolt on the carpet or laid it on the carpet, and the fibre that you found has simply come from that."

"Look, Ant, we'll have to go back to the study and check this out. Come on."

"Your wish is my command."

Back at the study, they opened the door and went inside. "Look at that," said Ant holding the tweezers close to the carpet; "it looks to be the same colour. What we'll have to do is take a sample from the edge of the carpet. Look after this fibre and pass me some scissors."

Elaine did this.

Anthony cut some fibres from the carpet close to the wall. "Right, Elaine, let's go to John Peet's office."

"Why do we need to go there?"

"To see if we can find some envelopes."

They entered John Peet's office. From a drawer, they took two envelopes. "Put the fibre in one of them, Elaine, and mark it 'A'. I'll put the ones from the carpet in the other envelope and mark it 'B'."

After this, Anthony took out his notebook and wrote in it: 'A' equals fibre, 'B' equals carpet pile."

"Right, Elaine, let's get out of here before someone else comes, and we have to find another excuse as to why we're here."

CHAPTER TWENTY ONE
Suspects

"What do you think of my theory now that you have actually done it yourself, Anthony?"

"I have to admit that it certainly is feasible, and I haven't forgotten the fibre that was stuck on the bolt, that might prove to be most important."

"Having said all that, we can't just go to the police with this; what we'll do is make some discreet enquiries, and see what information we can glean, as to who might have a motive for killing Brett."

"Just how do you propose to do that?"

"Well, I thought that as Aunt Norah knows most of the people who were at the party that fateful night; after all, she has worked at Northrop House for the last thirty years or so; that we could start with her."

"You can't just go to your Aunt Norah and start asking her all these questions or she'll want to know why you are asking them, and at this stage you can hardly tell her that we think Brett has been murdered."

"No, you're quite right. I was hoping that you might question Aunt Norah. Well I didn't really mean question her just like that. What I meant was that you should engage her in conversation and just casually ask a relevant question or two. You know what I mean."

"I see, so you expect me to do all the detective work, do you?"

"Not really. Oh, you know you'd be good at it, Elaine," Anthony wheedled.

"You're a right old soft soaper. You know how to get round me, don't you?"

"I knew you would. You're a little love."

By now they had reached Standish and he drew the car to a halt outside his home. Anthony held the car door open for Elaine to alight.

"Still the gentleman I see; what are you after?"

"I'm not after anything, Elaine, darling."

"Oh, yes you are," remarked Elaine with that sweet smile on her face once more.

"I'm very pleased that you agreed to pump...I mean subtly question Aunt Norah for information."

Anthony let them in with his latchkey. They heard voices coming from the Lounge. They entered, his mother looked up.

"I didn't expect to see you two here today."

"We just thought we'd come and see you." He looked towards his aunt, "Hello, Aunt Norah."

"Hello, what have you two been up to then?"

"Up to, what do you mean?" asked Anthony.

"Well," Elaine broke in, "Anthony and I have been discussing Brett's suicide and what we were saying was that at the inquest the coroner asked about Brett's mental attitude. Did he seem suicidal? And everyone who was questioned on that stressful day, including you, Norah agreed that they had no reason to believe that he would commit suicide as he seemed perfectly normal."

"So where does that lead us?" asked Jane.

"Well," said Anthony, "where, indeed!"

"You surely don't think it involved any foul play?" remarked Jane.

Anthony and Elaine looked at each other. "Well, Mum..."

"You do! Don't you? But who would want to kill him?"

Norah looked thoughtful. "Well, now you come to mention it. I shouldn't really be saying this, but it's well known that Alan Kay had a good reason."

Elaine nodded. "Do you know anyone else that might have a grievance against Brett?"

Norah bit her lip. The silence was deafening..."Well, where do you want me to begin?"

Jane raised her eyebrows. "So you think there may be others who wouldn't mind seeing Brett dead?"

"More than that, there were one or two who wouldn't mind doing the deed, I'll be bound."

"So who for instance, do you mean?"

"You wouldn't know this, Elaine; but you know, Anthony, what Brett was like with the ladies. At one time he was seeing Margaret Johnson, and Oliver could be Brett's. Then he threw her over for Alice Bentham, before dropping Alice for Sandra Kay. And he'd had numerous other affairs as well, and you know what they say, 'hell hath no fury like a woman scorned'. Apart from love affairs, Brett caused the accident that crippled Bill Johnson. So Frank might have more than one good reason; and I'm sure Margaret Johnson was still in love with Brett."

"One thing we mustn't overlook is just how he was killed; a massive overdose of insulin, who had access to that?" Anthony asked.

"Alice is on insulin as I'm sure you know and Dr.Hardman prescribed it, and got it for her," put in Norah.

"I hope you're not suggesting that my granddad killed Brett; he's a doctor and has taken an oath to save lives not take them," retorted Elaine, her face as black as thunder, her lips tightening as she said it.

"Well, it's true what I said, you can't deny that, Elaine, doctor or not."

"All the same, I know my granddad and he is no murderer, and further more what motive could he have for killing Brett?"

"John Peet is going out with Alice Bentham, isn't he, Aunt Norah?" Anthony asked, changing the subject, in an attempt to calm Elaine down.

"Yes, John and Alice are seeing each other."

"Just a minute, aren't we forgetting something here, wasn't Brett found dead in a room, the door of which was bolted on the inside and had to be broken into?" Jane asked.

Anthony and Elaine looked at each other, but said nothing...

"Yes, that's right, Jane, what about that Anthony?" Norah said.

He lit a cigarette... "We were only discussing what was said at the inquest, that's all."

"We'll have to be going shortly, Anthony."

"Yes, we will have to go, I'm afraid." Anthony went over and kissed his aunt's cheek.

"Do I not get a kiss then?" His mother asked.

Anthony went over and gave his mum a kiss on the cheek also, "See you later."

Elaine also gave Jane a kiss, and going over to Norah put her arms around her, "I'm sorry I raised my voice to you about my granddad."

"Oh, don't worry about that, I didn't mean that your granddad was in any way involved in this sordid affair, ok."

Elaine smiled as she drew away, "Thank you, Norah for that."

CHAPTER TWENTY TWO
Love Blossoms

They got into Anthony's car and drove off in the direction of Pepper Lane.

"Alone at last, well, Sexton, I think we almost made a pig's ear out of that subtle, attempt to glean some covert information about Brett's death."

"What do you mean?"

"Well, it came out rather abruptly, didn't it?"

"It had the desired effect; we got what we wanted to know, didn't we?"

"Yes, I do have to admit that much, but for a minute or so I thought Aunt Norah would have gone up the wall."

"Well, she didn't, in fact she seemed only too keen to put in her two-penn'orth."

"Ok, I suppose you're right."

"As usual," smiled Elaine, what now, then?"

"When we get back to your house I think we should make out a list of the people who may have good reason to kill Brett Northrop."

Elaine opened the front door of her home and they went inside. As she had expected, her mother, Rachael, was out; she usually went shopping in Wigan on a Thursday. Her dad, George Blake, an accountant, worked in Chorley. So they had the house to themselves. "Would you like a brew, Ant?"

"I wouldn't mind, tea, please."

"I'll get you some paper and a pen so you can write down that list."

"It's ok, I have a notebook."

"It's not for you, it's for me, I want a copy too."

"Oh all right, then, Sexton, I'll make a list for you as well."

She brought the teas through and sat beside him on the sofa. Anthony took out his fountain pen. "Right, what did Aunt Norah say?"

"Alan Kay: Brett was having an affair with his wife, Sandra.

Frank Johnson: Brett had an affair in the past with his wife, Margaret; and was responsible for the accident which crippled Bill Johnson, Frank's father.

Margaret Johnson: still secretly in love with Brett.

Alice Bentham: (on insulin) thrown over for Sandra.

John Peet: courting Alice."

He put his arms around her and cuddled her, whispering in her ear, "Anthony is courting Elaine."

She moved her cheek to his, and he bent his head and kissed her, her mouth opening beneath his. His hand touched her breast. "I'm sorry," he said, "I shouldn't have done that."

"Why ever not, it's ok?"

"Well, I don't want to take advantage of you. I love you, you know."

Elaine smiled happily. "Do you?"

"I certainly do."

"Well, you wouldn't be taking advantage of me, as I love you a lot, too."

"Do you love me as much as I love you?"

"Of course I do, Ant."

Encouraged, he continued to explore her breast.

"Let's go upstairs," she whispered, excited by his attention.

He looked surprised. "I don't think we should," he said.

"We'd be much more comfortable on my bed."

He chuckled. "You're a little temptress."

"It's only because I love you so much, Ant. So is it yes?"

"It certainly is. I'm only flesh and blood. No man could turn down an offer like that from someone as wonderful as you."

He took her hand and pulled her up from the sofa and they went upstairs and into Elaine's bedroom. They sat on the bed and started kissing again. Somehow, their clothing was discarded. He lay on top of her still kissing and fondling her.

She ran her fingers over his chest. "What a lovely hairy chest you've got, it's all curly. She twisted a curl around her finger.

Suddenly she heard the front door open. Elaine pushed him off her. "Mum! She's back early."

He groaned, "Oh, no!"

She pushed him towards the wardrobe. "Hide in there!"

As he moved towards it, he stubbed his toe on the dressing table. "Ouch! Damn and blast!"

"Shush! Get into the wardrobe." She threw his clothes in after him and closed the door.

"It's dark in here," he complained.

"Quiet! Mum will hear you." She scrambled into her dress and hastily fastened the buttons, before hurrying down the stairs. She opened the front door and then shut it with a bang.

Her mother, an older version of Elaine with wisps of greying hair amongst the gold was unpacking groceries in the kitchen. She looked up. "Has Anthony gone?" she asked.

"Yes." She didn't like lying, especially to her mother, but she couldn't tell the truth, could she? "He had just remembered an appointment; and had to dash off, he said that he was sorry that he didn't have time to say goodbye."

Her mother nodded. A few moments later, she said, "I'm going to do a spot of weeding in the back garden. Would you like to help me, Elaine?"

"I will in a minute, there's just something I have to do first."

"All right, then." Her mother put on her gardening gloves and went outside.

Elaine ran upstairs and let Anthony out of the wardrobe. He had managed to dress himself despite being in a dark enclosed space.

"The coast is clear. Mum's in the back garden."

He quickly kissed her cheek and ran down the stairs; followed by Elaine. "I'll see you tomorrow afternoon about two o'clock," she said. She let him out of the front door and breathed a sigh of relief. She went back into the kitchen and found herself some gardening gloves and joined her mother in the back garden.

As he drew away from the house, he thought that Elaine's mother appearing as she had was just as well. He wouldn't have liked to have got Elaine pregnant. He'd no contraceptives with him...he'd not thought that their relationship would move on so quickly. He loved Elaine Veronica Blake too much to see her shamed in that sort of way.

CHAPTER TWENTY THREE
A Walk In The Park

The following morning, Anthony went into work for a few hours.

"Good morning, William, I was wondering if you could do me a big favour and pull a few strings for me."

"Strings, what sort of strings?"

"Well, I can't go into any great details yet; but I want a small fibre checking against some other fibres to see if they are the same. Do you think you could arrange that? I'd be very grateful if you could."

"Sounds very mysterious, what's it all about?"

"Well, depending on the result it might not amount to anything. At the moment it's just a theory, but you'll get to know if anything positive comes from it."

"I'll see what I can do; have you got it with you?"

"No, but if you can arrange it, I'll bring it in to you, ok."He left the office at two o'clock and set off to pick Elaine up at Pepper Lane. He arrived outside her house at two forty pm.

"You're late, Mark Anthony," she said, as she got into the car.

"I'm sorry I'm late...My word you do look stunning," he wheedled.

"There you go, soft soaping again."

"No, I really mean it, you do look beautiful."

"Well, thank you, Anthony, where are we going?"

"I thought we might go to Astley Park. I called in at home and Mum made some ham sandwiches, a thermos flask of coffee and half a homemade sponge cake for us; and she sends her love. That's why I was so late."

"Oh, Ant, darling, you're forgiven. I would love a picnic in the park."

"Have you got the envelopes with you?" He asked, relating to her that he had put the wheels in motion to get the fibre checked out.

"No, they're at home in a safe place."

"I'll have to pick them up when we get back, I'll need to take them into work with me, probably on Monday."

"Let's look at this logically, "we want to know the truth, don't we?"

"Yes. We certainly do," replied Anthony.

"First of all; what if the fibre matches the carpet pile, what then?"

"If the fibres match, then we have no real reason to think of Brett's death as anything but suicide."

"That's the worst case scenario from my point of view as I am convinced that he was murdered. Call it woman's intuition call it what you like, but I think that there are too many things pointing to it, for it to be coincidence," Elaine expressed, "and what if the fibres do not match?"

"If the fibres don't match, then all we have at best is circumstantial evidence that he was murdered."

145

Anthony stopped the car outside the gates and they walked together hand-in-hand into the park.

"Circumstantial evidence won't be enough to go to the police with, will it, Ant?"

"Not really without anything more to go on."

"What about all the suspects that we have?"

"That's just what they are, suspects, its proof we need."

"Who do you think might have done it, if he was murdered?"

"Well of the six possible people; who we think could have killed him, we can rule out Bill Johnson as he is in a wheel chair, and more importantly was taken home before Brett died. So we're left with five and that is assuming that it was not someone else entirely. I have to say, I personally think that Alan Kay has the strongest motive simply because his wife's affair with Brett was ongoing at the time of his death; but of course, I could be wrong."

"What do you think, Sexton?"

"I have been thinking about this, and I've come up with two questions, so to speak. Was he killed by one person or two? If, as you think, Alan Kay did it, then he probably worked alone. If say, Frank Johnson killed him, did he work alone or did Margaret help him? Or did Margaret do it by herself? Then, there's Alice Bentham, Brett dropped her in favour of Sandra, and you heard what your aunt said, 'Hell hath no fury like a woman scorned' and John Peet is courting her; so did either or both of them do it; what do you say to that?"

146

"I say all this work is making me hungry. Let's go and get the picnic basket from the car and have something to eat."

Back at the car, Anthony opened the boot and lifted out the basket.

"Where's the blanket?" She asked.

"What blanket?"

"That's typical of a man! I'm not sitting on the grass in this dress and getting grass stains all over it, Ant."

"Oh, of course not; I never intended for us to do that; we will go and sit in the summerhouse." He said wheedling again.

On entering the summerhouse, he took a clean handkerchief from his pocket and dusted the seat where Elaine was going to sit.

"Why, thank you, Anthony, still, the gentleman I see. Now, getting back to this mystery," she remarked. "Who ever did kill him must have got hold of the insulin somehow. So does that not point to Alice or Alice and John?"

"Well, I don't want to upset you, so don't go off at the deep end; but your granddad did supply Alice with it, didn't he?"

"Yes, but..."

"Let me finish please; so if he had insulin in his bag then anyone could have taken some from it..."

"You mean at the party?"

"Well, at the party, yes, but maybe if he went anywhere else even before the night of the party, and let's say he did not lock his bag, then someone could have removed an ampoule without his knowledge."

147

"Let's go and see Granddad straight away."

"Let me finish my cake first."

They hurriedly put away their picnic things; Elaine practically ran back to the car.

"Hold your horses a minute." He grabbed her arm. "Don't you think we'd better wait until we get the results of the fibre test?"

"Why wait?"

"Well, suppose the results show that the fibre came from the carpet? We'll really be wasting our time and your granddad's, too."

Elaine reluctantly agreed.

They got into the car and twenty minutes later, were back at Elaine's house.

"Don't let me go without those envelopes, will you."

"No, I won't."

"Are you coming in for a brew?"

"Yes, why not?"

They went indoors, Elaine made them a drink and they sat down on the sofa.

"I can't wait to get the results of the fibre back; I'm convinced it won't match the carpet pile," she remarked.

"Don't be too disappointed if they do match, will you? They did look the same in colour. While we're on this subject, you had better give me those envelopes so we don't forget them."

Elaine dashed off upstairs, and came back a minute or so later with the two envelopes, handing them over to Anthony, she said, "Don't lose them, will you?"

"I'll guard them with your life, my love."

"You mean your life."

"I said your life," he repeated.

"Ah ha, very funny Ant, you'll think so if you do lose them."

They locked in an embrace, and kissed each other goodnight.

A worn out Anthony left Elaine's home and drove the short distance back to his home in Standish.

CHAPTER TWENTY FOUR
The Body In The Woods

Sandra was up early on the Saturday and got through quite a few chores, to keep her busy and get her mind off the recent traumatic events, and also to keep herself out of Alan's way. She left the house with Rex on his lead and walked down Wood Lane, a walk that she'd taken many times before. Rex barked excitedly at being out in the open air. Crossing the road, she walked across the field towards the pit, known locally as The Flood. She walked around it until she came to the woods and entered them. Seeing the leafy trees and wild flowers, and hearing birdsong, somehow lightened her mood and eased the distress of her recent arguments with Alan, or rather, his with her. She bent and let Rex off his lead and he scampered away. She walked on, feeling that this exercise had to be of benefit to her.

Then, to her astonishment, from behind a bush, loomed a face she knew only too well...

***

Alan Kay had been brooding over the affair for some time. There was a loud knocking at the door, he went to answer it. "Hold on, I'm coming, you've no need to knock the door down." He opened the door and gasped at the sight of two police officers. "What, the...!" burst out Alan.

The elder of the two, removed his helmet.

"Mr. Kay? I`m sorry, sir, to have to tell you; but we believe that the body of a young woman that has just been found is probably your wife."

"What! It can`t be, where did you find her? The last time I saw her she was taking Rex for a walk."

"And how long ago was that?"

"I don`t know. He rubbed his hands through his hair. "It can`t be her, it can`t be!"

"You`ll have to come and identify the woman. She`s at the hospital morgue. We were informed by a man who was also walking his dog, that he had seen a female body in the undergrowth. A dog, a golden Labrador was whining, by the body.

"But, how did she die? What makes you think it`s Sandra?"

"Because she`d a brooch on her coat, with 'Sandra' on it."

Alan bit his lip. "I gave her that brooch." With effort, he pulled himself together. "It can`t be her. It just can`t! There must be millions of women called Sandra."

"That might be, but the dog has a collar with this address on it."

Alan flinched, as he noticed a van draw up and another policeman taking Rex from it. Rex spotting Alan; barked excitedly, "C'mon Rex, come here," the dog jumped up at him. "Good boy, Rex, sit," the dog sat wagging his tail, half whining half growling.

"You will have to come with us to identify the body."

"What now? I can't come now. What about Rex? There's nobody to look after him."

The younger policeman raised his eyebrows "We'll see to him, sir, don't worry about that."

Alan got into the police car and Rex began to bark as the car drove away.

The mortuary attendant pulled back the sheet. Reluctantly, Alan moved forward. He looked down at the waxen body before him. Could this be Sandra, this doll-like effigy with pale skin and pennies over her eyes lying dead on the slab?

"Good heavens it's her!"

"This is your wife, sir, is it Sandra Kay of No.12 Wood Lane, Wrightington Bar?" asked the more senior looking one of the two policemen.

Alan nodded his head "Yes, it is Sandra, why; who would do such a thing?"

"Are you all right, sir," asked the mortuary attendant as he pulled the sheet back over Sandra's face.

"I'm shocked I...I can't believe it who on earth would want to kill her."

"Well, that's what we need to find out; would you mind coming down to the station with us so we can ask you a few questions."

"What! You don't think I did it, do you?"

"No, nothing like that, it's just a matter of course, a formality, that's all."

"What, right now?"

"You wouldn't mind, would you, sir?"

Alan winced; visibly shaking, he nodded.

The interview room at Standish Police Station felt cold and Alan was trembling, despite the day being quite warm.

"Now, then, sir; what can you tell us that may be of help in trying to find out who killed your wife?"

"In what way, do you mean?" Ill at ease, Alan rubbed his hands together.

"For instance, did Sandra have any enemies, anyone who may have wanted to see her dead?"

"See her dead? Why no everybody got on well with her, she had no enemies."

"She must have had at least one, sir; she didn't die of natural causes."

Alan cringed at the words.

"What was your relationship with her like, was it ok?"

"Yes, it was ok, we got on, we had our differences just like any married couple."

"When did you last see Sandra alive?"

"As I have already told you, it was when she took Rex out for a walk, this morning."

"About what time was that?"

"I suppose, about eight thirty, I think."

"So the last time that you saw her alive was at eight thirty this morning, is that correct?"

"Yes."

"How would you describe her mental attitude, was she in good spirits or did she seem depressed at all?"

"No, she seemed perfectly normal to me."

"And you don't know of anyone who might have a reason to kill her?"

"No."

"Did anyone see you; or did you see anyone before eight thirty this morning who can verify your whereabouts?"

Alan thought for a moment or two then answered, "No, no one saw me and I didn't see anyone either."

"So you don't have anyone who can collaborate what you say, as to your whereabouts before eight thirty?"

"There's no one."

"Well, I think that's all for the moment, Mr. Kay, you can go now, we'll be getting in touch with you again, later."

Alan left the police station and made his way home.

"They didn't believe me I'm sure, not for one moment," Alan muttered to himself.

CHAPTER TWENTY FIVE
Hanging By A Thread

Anthony pushed open the office door and walked in. It was a warm Monday morning; he removed his coat and hung it on one of the coat hooks, at the same time, he took the envelopes from his inside pocket.

He sat down at his desk and placed the envelopes carefully in front of him. He hoped that William Stone would not be in late, he was almost as excited as Elaine was to get to know if the fibres matched or not.

He did not have to wait for very long. William entered the office, "Good morning, Anthony.

"Good morning, William, I've brought those fibres in for you as we arranged.

"Good, I rang the Laboratory on Friday and they said to drop it in today and they will test them for us."

"When can we expect to get the results, do you know?"

"When they are ready; it all depends on how busy they are at the Lab. We can't demand a quick return. But if it will help, I'll tell them it's urgent."

"Oh, thank you," said Anthony, as he handed over the envelopes.

Anthony was deep in thought, but the telephone ringing brought him back to the present. "Hello; Sergeant and Stone, Anthony Hilton speaking."

"Hi, Ant, it's me, Elaine."

"Hiya sweetheart, how are you?"

"Listen, Anthony, I've just heard that Sandra Kay has been found dead."

"What! Where was she found?"

"Apparently her body was found in Long Meadow Woods, some time on Saturday afternoon. She had been strangled, by all accounts. I can't tell you much more at the moment, but I'll see you this evening after work, ok?"

"All right, see you this evening, love you, bye." He put down the phone. "Good grief! Sandra murdered, I can hardly believe it."

He raced home after work and gulped down his tea. He quickly told his mother what Elaine had said, had a good wash, shave and change of clothing. He dashed off to her house.

She opened the door.

He kissed her lips, but he was too agog about the murder to get more passionate. "Well," he said, "has old Alan gone and strangled Sandra?"

"Well, possibly."

"Oh, by the way, with all the shocking news of Sandra's death, Elaine, darling; I completely forgot to tell you on the telephone this morning, William took the fibres into the Lab today. The results could be back tomorrow with a bit of good luck. William said he would tell them that it was urgent."

"That's good; I hope they are back tomorrow."

He frowned. "If the results of the fibre test indicate that Brett was murdered, could the same person have killed both of them?"

"I suppose so, and Alan has a good reason to kill both her and Brett," said Elaine.

"True!"

"But they could be two separate murders," said Elaine.

"What in a quiet place like Wrightington? This isn't America; you know we've not got gangsters behind every lamppost."

Thank goodness for that! Now, let's have a cup of tea and forget about murder for a bit – it makes me shiver!"

"Don't worry, darling, I'll look after you," said Anthony.

"I'll put the television on and see what's on. Where's the Radio Times?" She found it and looked up the programme for that evening. "Oh, no, it's only a Murder Mystery. We can't get away from it, can we?" They both fell about laughing at this.

They spent the rest of the evening in the company of Elaine's parents. They were chatting about things in general and about the murder of Sandra in particular.

"That was a horrible affair, the young woman who was murdered in the woods at Wrightington Bar." George commented.

"I didn't know her." Elaine's mother remarked. "I expect there will be something about it in the Observer on Thursday."

"Yes, it will probably be in the Wigan Observer." Elaine said, not wanting to get too involved with the details at that time.

"There are some terrible things going on in the world today," Rachael remarked.

"Yes," Anthony agreed "unfortunately, we see a lot of it in our profession."

"I'll bet you do, too. In a lot of these cases, the husband's done it," said George.

"Or, a lunatic, I read in The News of the World last Sunday about one who had escaped from Broadmoor and strangled three women before he was apprehended," Rachael added.

"That'd be a long way to come to here," said George.

"But not from Winwick Mental Asylum at Warrington," put in Rachael.

"Let's change the subject. Who's for Bridge?" George asked.

"That's a good idea," Elaine replied. "Come on, Ant, pull your chair up to the table and bring one for Mum, will you."

George and Anthony paired up, to play against the two women.

"Good grief; just look at the time, it's eleven fifty already, we'd better make this the last rubber; we'll never get up in the morning," Rachael yawned.

It was gone twelve twenty; already Tuesday by the time the game was over, the women having won.

Anthony gave Rachael a kiss on her cheek and said goodnight to her and George, who went straight upstairs to bed, leaving the two young ones to kiss and say goodnight to each other; after which Anthony left the house; thinking about whether or not, he would get the results in the morning as he drove home?

CHAPTER TWENTY SIX
Disappointment

Tuesday was rather cloudy and overcast with some drizzle, a change from the fine hot weather that they had enjoyed recently. It was already two thirty pm, and the weather matched Anthony's mood as he waited impatiently for the test results to come back. He had just finished typing up the report on the embezzlement case he had been working on.

Anthony looked at his watch again; just as the door opened; the time was four fifteen pm.

It was William, "Hello, Anthony; I've got that report from the Lab for you."

"Oh, great, what did they say?"

"I don't know it's sealed up, I just brought it straight here for you. I can't stop I'm picking my daughter up in ten minutes from the Technical College, I'll see you tomorrow, ok."

"Right see you in the morning; and thank you for getting this report for me."

"Glad to have been of service, goodnight," he said as he left; closing the door behind him. Anthony hurriedly, but carefully opened the A5 envelope He removed the document and unfolded it.

THE EVIDENCE RECOVERY UNIT (ERU)
MANCHESTER
TEXTILE CERTIFICATION

SERGEANT & STONE
39 WALLGATE
WIGAN
LANCASHIRE.

Test on textile fibres   11th August 1958

(A)	(B)
Sort: Multi Filament	Multi Filament
Colour.Red	Red/Crimson
Fibre Type Silk	Wool

A.Goodman.

Anthony's face lit up. "Well, just look at that, Elaine will be over the moon when I tell her," he said, talking to himself.

He reached out and took hold of the A5 envelope and put his hand inside. Pulling it open, he looked into it, "Good grief, where's the other envelopes? They're not here." The expression on his face changed to one of annoyance.

Anthony snatched up the telephone; and dialled '0', he listened intensely to the ringing tone...click.

"Hello, operator, can I help you?"

"Yes, will you put me through to The Evidence Recovery Unit in Manchester, please?"

160

"Just one moment please...I'm putting you through."

"Thank you."

From the other end of the line someone said, "Hello E.R.U."

"Oh, hello, it's Anthony Hilton, from Sergeant and Stone speaking. We had some fibres tested at your Lab yesterday and the results were picked up today by Mr. Stone. Unfortunately, the two envelopes containing the fibres; marked 'A' and 'B' have not been returned with the report. Do you still have them, please?"

"Just a minute I'll have a look."..."Hello I can't see anything of them here; Arthur Goodman did the test; but he went home a bit before you rang. He will be in tomorrow; you can speak to him then. My name's Shirley."

"Oh, dear me, it's the envelope marked with the letter 'A' that's important. It contained a single fibre about half an inch or so long, and we desperately need that fibre back."

"Did you tell Arthur that when the sample was brought in?"

"Well, it was William who took it in to you and I was not with him at the time so I don't know if he did or didn't tell him."

"I'm sorry, but I can't do anything now until tomorrow; I'll speak to him then and get him to ring you back about it, all right?"

"I suppose it will have to be, as you say you can't do any more, but thanks for trying anyway, ok, goodbye." A dejected Anthony dropped the telephone down onto its cradle.

"Only a few minutes ago I was saying that Elaine would be over the moon with the results. Now, she'll kill me," he muttered. Not only did he hope to get the approval of Elaine, he also hoped that if the police realised that instead of a suicide the fibre proved that a murder had been committed, and his firm were impressed with what he had done, this might lead to him getting promotion from a junior to a senior detective, which of course, would mean a rise in his salary. More money would mean he could ask Elaine if she'd consider becoming Mrs Hilton.

That evening when he saw Elaine he gave her the good news that a favourable report had been returned to him showing the fibre was made of silk and the carpet fibres were wool.

"Great!" she said, kissing him on the cheek.

"Not great at all," he admitted; "they didn't return the envelopes with the report."

"What do you mean?"

"Well, Angel face, they've been left at the 'ERU' in Manchester as far as I know. Hopefully they'll turn up."

"Why shouldn't they turn up?"

"Well, to be honest with you I spoke to someone called Shirley and she said that a Mr. Goodman had done the test but he had gone home just before I rang. She looked for the envelopes but couldn't find them, and she said she'd ask him in the morning and get him to ring me back."

"Well, Ant, if they don't appear you'll be shot at dawn!"

The following morning, Anthony went into work living in the hopes that the envelopes would be found. He sat at his desk with his eyes glued to the telephone. When it finally rang he leapt up knocking his chair over in the process. He snatched up the telephone. "Hello, Sergeant and Stone, Anthony Hilton speaking."

From the other end of the line a voice said, "Hello, it's Arthur Goodman, from ERU. I believe you've been very concerned about the envelopes that came here with your samples in. Don't worry; I had locked them in the drawer for safe keeping. Unfortunately, the Report was sent out without them. I will post them to you immediately. You should get them in the morning."

"Thank you very much for that, Mr. Goodman. I'll look forward to getting them tomorrow." Thank God for that, I'm off the hook, he thought. "Goodbye, Mr. Goodman, and thank you once again."

He picked up the chair and flopped down into it. "Whew!" He wiped his brow with his hand. Things are looking up at last.

CHAPTER TWENTY SEVEN
Doctor Hardman's Confession

That evening Anthony met Elaine outside her home in Pepper Lane. "Hello, darling, Angel face."

"Hi, Anthony, how are you?"

"A lot better than I was. This morning I had a phone call from Arthur Goodman and he's posted the fibres to me this morning, I should get them tomorrow morning."

"Great!" she said. "Does this mean we can go to Granddad's now to ask him about the insulin in his bag?"

"Let's be off," he replied.

They drove to Standish and parked up outside of Dr Hardman's surgery. Elaine looked at her watch. "Perfect timing Ant, its six fifteen and Granddad will have just finished his surgery, so we should catch him straight away."

He held the car door open for her to alight.

They climbed the steps and went round to the side of the house and rang the bell.

The doctor's housekeeper, a widow in her fifties answered the door.

"Hello, Mrs Williams. We've come to see Granddad."

"Oh, hello, Elaine, are you all right, love?"

"Yes, this is my boyfriend, Anthony."

She put out her hand and Anthony shook it. "Pleased to meet you; Mrs Williams."

"Your granddad's in the lounge go through." She opened the door wider and they went inside.

Dr Hardman's face lit up. He rose from his armchair and threw his arms around her. "Hello, Anthony," he said. He smiled warmly at them. "To what do I owe this pleasure?"

"It's a rather delicate matter, Granddad."

"You don't mean...?"

"No, no, it's not that." Elaine laughed.

"Anyway, take the weight off your feet both of you. Sit down and tell me all about it."

They sat side by side on the settee and looked uncertainly at each other. "It's rather a long story, Granddad. Do you remember the night of the party?"

"How could I forget it?"

"Well," said Elaine. She related to him what she and Anthony had discovered... bringing her granddad up to date.

Dr Hardman frowned. "So where is all this leading us?"

"What we want to know. Did you ever leave your bag unlocked whilst unattended, from the time you put Alice Bentham on insulin?"

"I've got a confession to make, Anthony," said Dr Hardman. "Sometime ago, before Alice Bentham went on insulin, I lost the key to my bag. Consequently, I have been unable to lock my bag since then."

"Oh, I see what you mean; do you know if any of the insulin ampoules were missing from your bag?" asked Anthony

"Mmm... to tell the truth I honestly don't know. I got a fresh batch from the chemist's on the Thursday the same day I ran into your Aunt Norah across the road from here. But I can't remember if I had two or three ampoules left in my bag. But on that fateful night there were only two in my bag; after the discovery of Brett's body."

"Had you been anywhere else; with the insulin still in your bag before the party?"

He rubbed his chin. "Let me see; I did make a few visits to different patients but none of them were at the party. Except I called in on young Oliver Johnson, he had Rubella."

"Did you leave your bag unattended at all?"

"Not that I know...Oh, yes, I went into the kitchen to wash my hands and left it briefly in the hallway. It was whilst I was drying my hands that Frank came into the kitchen; he had just come in through the front door and through the hallway."

"Would he have had time to go into your bag and remove an ampoule?"

"Yes, probably, I don't know how long he had been in there."

"Do you think that he may have taken an ampoule from your bag?" asked his granddaughter.

"Well, now that is a question that I can't answer."

"So there was no other time that you left your bag unattended." Anthony put in.

"It was unattended at the party, of course. Your Aunt Norah said to leave it in her workroom as it would be safe in there.

I only brought the bag with me to the party because I had left word with the wife of a patient of mine who was very poorly; that I would be at Northrop House that evening, and that she should call me if her husband needed me at all."

"So when you arrived at Northrop who else was present when Aunt Norah told you to put your bag in the workroom?" Anthony asked.

"Let me see, yes, there was Margaret Johnson and Bill, and young Oliver, oh and Alice Bentham, of course."

"So at least four people; knew that you had left your bag in the workroom."

"I think we can leave Oliver out of this, can't we," remarked Elaine.

"Yes," they were all in agreement about that.

"I think that we can almost rule out Bill Johnson as well,can't we, as he is in a wheelchair," remarked the doctor.

"I don't know about that, he could still have gone into the workroom and got into your bag, wheelchair or not," retorted Anthony.

"Well, I suppose so," replied the doctor.

The lounge door opened and Mrs. Williams entered "Would anyone like some tea?"

"Yes, please, that would be lovely," Elaine expressed.

Mrs Williams hurried off and was back in a few minutes with a tray of tea things which she laid out on the table along with some biscuits. "Tuck in, they're my homemade shortbreads baked with real butter."

"They sound delicious," Anthony exclaimed.

167

Everyone enjoyed the wonderful biscuits, and Elaine asked Mrs William's for the recipe for her mother.

She put down her cup. "Well, Granddad, what do you think? Do we have enough to go to the police with? Or do you think that the circumstantial evidence we have is not enough for the police to do anything with?"

"I know that the evidence you have is only circumstantial but ask yourself this question, is it my duty to report this to the authorities? Even, if nothing ever comes from it."

"If you put it like that," said Elaine, "then I suppose we should go to the police. What do you think about Sandra being murdered? Do you think her husband did it? And if so, could he also have killed Brett?"

"Perhaps, but we can't just jump to conclusions, anyway, that is for the police to decide, not us. And they haven't arrested Alan so far as we know, although he does have a strong motive, even for both murders."

"I'll tell you what has just occurred to me. Do you remember when we bumped into Brett at the Post Office, Granddad?"

"Yes, I remember seeing him at the Post Office; why?

"Do you remember giving him some sleeping tablets?"

"Yes."

"If he had taken those tablets, how would they have affected him if someone had injected insulin into him?"

"Well, the tablets would make him drowsy, of course, but would not in any way interfere with the action of the insulin which undoubtedly killed him."

"But surely he would wait until he got to bed before he took sleeping tablets?"

"Not necessarily, Anthony," said Doctor Hardman. "The tablets wouldn't work immediately. He could have taken them a while before retiring."

"Right; so are you off tomorrow to the Police Station when you get the fibre back?"

"And what do you think this fibre might be from?"

"I don't know. All I know is that it is a red silk fibre."

Anthony and Elaine agreed to meet outside of the Bank Chambers in Wigan the following evening after work to go to the Police Station with the fibre; providing, of course, that he had received it by then.

"I will ring you at work and make the final arrangements with you tomorrow. Well, goodbye, Dr. Hardman and thank you for your advice," Anthony said, as he shook the doctor's hand.

Elaine gave her granddad a big kiss and a hug and they left the doctor's house.

CHAPTER TWENTY EIGHT
Confusion

The alarm clock ringing brought Anthony back to the land of the living. He yawned and stretched out his arms. The clock said it was seven fifteen. He got out of bed and went for a wash and shave.

"Your breakfast is ready," his mother shouted up the stairs.

"I'm coming," he replied.

"Boiled egg and toast," Jane said, putting the plate in front of him.

Anthony hurriedly ate his breakfast, and set off to go to work. He arrived on time and entered in to what would prove to be a long drag. The morning went by at a snail's pace, Anthony feeling no interest in the work he was doing. The worst part was that when the post arrived there was no letter from the ERU, a big disappointment to him. He had been looking forward to getting the fibre back and what would Elaine say?

The afternoon was no better and he was getting irritable. He was just about to ring Elaine and tell her the bad news when the second post fell through the letterbox, and there was an envelope from the ERU. Anthony opened the letter and inside was a packet containing the fibre. He could scarcely contain himself and rang Elaine immediately to give her the good news.

"Hiya sweetheart, the fibre has just arrived, so I'll pick you up outside the Bank Chambers as arranged after work, and we will go to the police with it."

"That's wonderful, Anthony. So I'll see you at five thirty. Love you, sweetheart; bye."

"I love you too; see you at five thirty, bye."

What a change that made to Anthony's day; he was like a new man, the work he was doing became light and easy and what's more the time past so quickly that the afternoon flew by and it was time to finish work.

Elaine was already waiting for him outside of The Bank Chambers.

"Jump in," he held the door open for her.

"Hi, Ant," she sat down beside him; she leaned across and kissed him, "let's be off."

They drove the short distance to the Police Station with its familiar blue lamp. He parked the car and they went inside.

The desk sergeant; a portly man in his fifties with greying hair; stood behind the desk. "Hello, Anthony, what brings you here?"

"Hello, Sergeant Smith; is Detective Chief Inspector Price in?"

"Yes, do you want to see him? I'll see if he's free." He left the desk and went through to the offices.

"I wonder what they will make of this story," Elaine whispered.

"We'll soon find out," Anthony said.

Sergeant Smith came back in. "He'll see you in a moment; he's just on the telephone."

A few minutes later, the door opened and D.C.I. Price walked in. "Come on, through to my office." He went and sat down at his desk. "Have a seat," he beckoned, "now what can I do for you?"

"On the 19th of July a party was held at Northrop House, Wrightington Bar. During the party it was discovered that the owner, Brett Northrop was dead in his study, the door of which was bolted on the inside. On the night in question, Detective Inspector Tom Grimshaw and Sergeant Dick Rigby from Standish Police Station were called in and did the investigations into what appeared to be a suicide... Anthony continued to relate the rest of the story and their findings to him. A statement of facts was drawn up which both Elaine and Anthony signed.

"Leave it with me and I'll look into it," said the D.C.I.

"Thank you," said Anthony.

"I'll keep you informed should anything develop."

The day following their visit to the Police Station was somewhat overcast.

The telephone ringing at A.J.Jones solicitor's office brought Elaine scurrying back to her desk. "Hello, A.J.Jones, Elaine Blake speaking... Oh, it's you, Anthony."

"Aunt Norah rang me a few minutes ago and what do you think?"

"I don't know, what should I think?"

"She told me that Alan Kay has been arrested on suspicion of murdering Sandra, and has been taken to Standish Police Station."

"Hmm, so they must think he could have done it?"

"Don't know."

"With it looking like Brett was murdered, it could have been Alan that did both murders."

Anthony chuckled. "Don't get too carried away, Elaine, it could have been some maniac that did poor Sandra in."

"They could have found some more evidence as regards Sandra."

"We'll have to see how things pan out. Now, Angel face, what are we doing tonight? Is it a ride in the car and a drink at a pub, or do you fancy the cinema?"

You know what I fancy, Anthony."

From the other end of the line came a gasp.

"It's not what you're thinking, cheeky blighter; it's a meal in a nice restaurant."

"Yes, that's just what I was thinking. A restaurant it is then!"

"Good! Don't forget your wallet, Anthony."

"I won't!" He laughed.

"Cheerio, then, Ant. See you soon." She put the phone down.

Well, that's something, isn't it, she thought.

***

Back in Northrop House Norah was in her Sitting Room quietly thinking to herself. The same words kept running through her mind, there's something wrong, she had been going through Brett's personal things putting away his clothes and such

173

like, tidying up in general; his wallet and cigarette case, it was while she was looking at his glasses; there were two pairs, she had discovered that one pair had plain glass lenses which did not make any sense as Brett could not see a thing without his glasses, what was his reason for the plain glass for lenses? Something's not right. She couldn't put her finger on it and it was worrying her. She'd had these thoughts for some time but had said nothing to anyone about them; should she confront the person who could perhaps answer her question or not? What would be the outcome if she did? It frightened her. She would have liked to discuss it with someone, but who could she trust? Better not to, better to keep it to herself, at least for the time being. Although at the same time she wanted to bring it out into the open.

CHAPTER TWENTY NINE
A Shocking State Of Affairs

John Peet had just started to type, when he thought he heard what sounded like a scream. He looked at his watch; it was almost brew time. He strained his ears, but there was only silence.

He got up and left his office heading for the kitchen. As he approached the kitchen door he heard a strange sound coming from within, a noise like someone choking. He pushed the door open and a horrific scene met his eyes. Peter Northrop had Norah by the throat and was strangling her.

"What on earth are you doing?" shouted John as he tried to intervene; grabbing hold of Peter's arms in an attempt to pull him off her. Peter lashed out, hitting John in the face, sending him reeling. He picked himself up and once again grabbed hold of Peter's arm, pulling with all his might, he managed to get one hand off Norah's throat. Peter wrenched himself from John's grasp and struck him another blow; "Ouch," but he managed to keep hold of him, both men went crashing onto the kitchen table, sending crockery and things flying onto the floor. Peter picking himself up turned scowling at John and ran off, through the door leading to the outside of the house, his face like thunder.

John immediately dashed across to see how Norah was. Only to be faced with a second shock. Norah's eyes were bulging from her head, her mouth all twisted, her right arm seemed lifeless and she was slumped to one side.

He rushed back to his office and phoned Dr.Hardman.

"Hello, Dr. Hardman's surgery, Olive speaking, what can I do for you?"

"Hello, can I speak to Dr. Hardman, please, it's urgent?"

"I'm sorry he's out on his rounds at the moment, can I take a message?

"You don't know where he is, do you?"

"No, I'm sorry, I don't, but he should be back shortly."

"When he gets back will you tell him to come to Northrop House, it's urgent, Norah Gray seems to have had some kind of stroke; or something; ok, thank you."

John put the phone down and hurried back to Norah to see if she was all right. He tried to make her as comfortable as possible, putting a cushion under her head; and then went back again to his office to phone for the police.

He dialled 999. A voice came on the line, "Emergency, which service do you require?"

"Police, please...and an ambulance, the housekeeper at Northrop House has been attacked and seems to have suffered a stroke."

"Northrop House and what is the address?"

"Carr House Lane, Wrightington Bar, near Wigan, could you please hurry? Norah seems to be in a bad way."

"Is the person who attacked her still at the house?"

"I don't know, he ran off outside and I haven't been out to see."

176

"The police and ambulance will be with you shortly."

"Thank you," John said and replaced the receiver.

To John; it seemed like a lifetime waiting for the services to come, although it was, in fact, only a few minutes. The ambulance was first to arrive.

"She's in here," John indicated the way in.

The ambulance men followed him into the kitchen, where Norah lay on the floor... "She's had a stroke all right and a bad one at that."

"Will she come round from it?" John enquired.

"I'm sorry, but we can't answer that; only time will tell."

They attended to her and quickly got her on to the stretcher and out to the ambulance. While Norah was being taken to Wigan Infirmary the police arrived. John told them what had happened. Frank Johnson also had come across to the house to see what was going on. "I saw Peter drive off like a madman."

"Which way did he go?" asked one of the policemen.

"'e went out down the right 'and side of the driveway, but I don't know which way 'e went after that."

"What was he driving?"

"A Jaguar MK1 Royal blue saloon; it had been his deceased brother's car," said John.

"Do you know the number of the car?"

"Yes, its 357 BNF."

"Have you any idea where he may be going?"

"No, I haven't, have you any idea where he could be heading for, Frank?"

"No, I don't, I didn't think 'e really knew anybody; 'e 'as only been 'ere about four or five weeks."

"I wonder why he attacked Norah like that, what could she have done to deserve it."

"We'll be in touch with you again later," remarked one of the policemen.

When they had left John went back inside. I'll have to let Jane and Anthony know, I'm not looking forward to that. Everyone is going to be very shocked to hear about it, he thought. Its Norah's sister, Jane, I'm most concerned about, they were very close.

Back in his office he looked up the number of Sergeant & Stone and was just about to dial it; when the doctor burst in. "When I heard what had happened I came as quick as I could; where is she?"

"Oh, Doctor Hardman, she's gone to hospital. When I couldn't get hold of you, I called the ambulance."

"How is she?"

"I'm afraid she's in a bad way, they said she's had a very bad stroke. But that is only half the story, Peter attacked her for God knows what reason?"

John brought him up to date with what had happened.

"Good heavens! I would imagine it was the attack that brought on the stroke."

"I was just about to ring Anthony at work about this, but..."

"Would you like me to do it?"

He heaved a sigh of relief. "Would you? I wasn't looking forward to imparting such news."

"I'm used to it. I'll call in on my way home."

Doctor Hardman pulled up outside Jane's house. I hope she's in, best to get it over with.

He knocked at the door. Jane opened it. "Doctor Hardman, I didn't expect you. Is there something wrong?"

"Unfortunately, yes. Can I come in?"

"Of course, you can." He followed her into the lounge and indicated an armchair. "Please sit down."

This she did, looking apprehensive.

"Prepare yourself for some bad news."

"Bad news, it's not Anthony, is it?"

"No, it isn't Anthony, I'm afraid it's your sister, Norah. I believe that she has had a bad stroke, and they have taken her to the Infirmary."

"Oh, dear me, I must go and see her. When did this happen?"

"I'm sorry to have to tell you this, but it is worse than that, Jane.

"What do you mean worse than that, what is it?"

"Peter Northrop attacked her, and John Peet fought him off otherwise he might have killed her."

"Peter! Why would Peter attack her? She thought the world of him."

"Yes, that's a good question, unfortunately one we can't answer at the moment; it's a mystery."

"I'll have to go and see her," Jane said, as she went out into the hall, reaching for her coat.

"I'll take you; if you like, I wouldn't mind seeing her myself."

"Oh that's kind of you." A tear rolled down her cheek.

The doctor drove them to Wigan Infirmary and they went inside.

At the desk Jane approached the receptionist. "I'm looking for Norah Gray, I'm her sister, I believe she was brought in earlier today, she's had a stroke. Can you tell me which ward she's on, please?"

"Ah, yes, she's in Intensive Care, ward three."

On reaching the bed, although she knew her sister was in a bad way, the sight of Norah's condition still shocked her. Norah's eyes were wide open and she was staring as if she was blind. Her mouth all pulled down on the right hand side. Her right arm also was hanging lifelessly.

CHAPTER THIRTY
Old Haunts Revisited

Peter's foot was hard down on the accelerator; the speedometer was reading ninety miles per hour as he approached Salford on the A580 East Lancs Road. He almost collided with a car coming the other way and just swerved in time. He hadn't wanted to hurt Norah, but he had no choice. She'd been good to them as boys, giving them cakes straight from the oven when they came home starving, from school. He and Brett had known her almost all of their lives.

He realised he would soon be on Broad Street A6 for Manchester, and would be happier then. As he approached the outskirts of Manchester he dropped his speed down to a steady thirty mph, I don't want to be pulled over for speeding, he thought. He'd planned to run the car into the back streets and then abandon it, and lose himself in the city.

The car shuddered, he realised that the petrol gauge was on empty. He had meant to get filled up earlier, but had forgotten to do it; he had not expected this to happen. The car shuddered once more and died. He was out of petrol.

He sat there, what should he do now? Should he leave the car and try to thumb a lift? As he was mulling this over, he heard the siren of a police car getting louder and louder, but to his relief it turned off down another road. This made his mind up for him.

He got out of the car and started walking. He heard a car approaching and stuck his thumb out, but the car carried on. Another car approached, but the same thing happened again. A third car approached, third time lucky, he thought, holding out his hand. This time the car stopped. "I've run out of petrol," he said. "You couldn't possibly run me to a garage?"

"Certainly," the man replied, "hop in."

At the garage, he approached the petrol attendant and explained what had happened. The attendant found him an empty can and put a gallon of petrol in it for him.

He started walking back towards his car, thumbing each car that passed him. Eventually, one pulled up for him. He explained that his car was down the road, and could the man give him a lift back. "I'll make it worth your while," he said.

The man nodded his agreement, and when they reached Peter's car he gave the man a ten shilling note. The man's face lit up. "Thank you, Squire," he said, pocketing the money. His car roared off.

Peter put the petrol into the tank, and set off to move the car into the back streets. While he didn't like the idea of leaving the car, he knew that sooner or later, the police, who must be looking for it, would find it. So better to abandon it now and proceed on foot.

Knowing Manchester as well as he did it was quite easy for him to decide just where to leave the car. A quiet street not too far to walk to a familiar small guest house, they'd used when he and his brother were young. He lifted the heavy lion's head knocker and knocked on the door. A grey-haired man about six feet tall with a handlebar moustache of the kind pilot's sported during the war appeared.

"Well, bless my soul, if it isn't Peter Northrop. How are you? You haven't been to see us for some time, come in."

"Hello, Eric. It's good to see you again, too."

They shook hands. "What will you have to drink, and would you like a cigarette?" Peter took one, and Eric lit it for him.

"Thank you, I'll have a coffee if I may."

"Coffee it is then.So what brings you to this neck of the woods?"

"I'm here on business for a day, or two, it may be longer."

"So how's old Brett going on? You used to be inseparable."

"I'm afraid Brett is no longer with us." He related how his brother had committed suicide a few weeks back.

Eric looked shocked. "Well, I'm sorry to hear that, it's so hard to believe that about Brett, knowing him as I did."

"Yes, it was a shock to all those who knew him, no one could hardly believe it."

Eric nodded.

"I'll just go and tell Mary you're here and she can get your usual room ready for you, I'm sure, she too, will be glad to see you." He left the room.

Peter looked round, it had been re-decorated since he was last here, but still bore a resemblance to the old place they used to stay at.

Eric returned, followed by Mary, who kissed Peter's cheek. "Lovely to see you again," she gushed. "The coffee won't be a moment. I was sorry to hear about Brett, Eric was just telling me all about it; it's shocking." She went out again.

"Have you any more guests in?"

"Yes," replied Eric, "two, a young woman and a commercial traveller. They're both out at the moment, but you'll see them later when we have our evening meal."

Mary brought his coffee which he drank.

A little while later she put her head round the door, "Your room's ready for you," she said.

He went upstairs and after having a wash, lay on the bed. He knew that dinner wouldn't be before seven o'clock so he had time for a snooze. But he couldn't sleep; his mind was too active because of what had happened that day. Although, he had some cash on him, he would have to get hold of some more and was considering his position. He did have his cheque book on him but dare he risk going to the bank with one made out to cash himself, and if so how much could he ask for without raising awkward questions? Or would it be better to go back to Northrop House in the dead of night, he had access to some money and clothing. Yes, that was the way to go as he would also need his passport if he was to get to Canada. That's settled then, he thought, in the early hours of the morning he would set of and be back before anyone was awake. It was time to go to dinner, he smartened himself up went down the creaky stairs and entered the Dining Room.

The other guests were already seated at the table. "Hello, I'm Peter; and you're...?" He said holding out his hand.

"I'm Charlotte, pleased to meet you."

"I'm Roger." They shook hands.

They all enjoyed an excellent meal and some good conversation, during which Peter said that he was going to take a stroll after dinner.

He made sure that he had his key with him, as he pulled the door shut behind him. A quick look round and he set off back to his car. He had to get some petrol, as the gallon put in earlier would not get him there and back. As he approached the car he saw a man in plain clothes apparently examining it. His heart leaped into his mouth, then he realised the man had only stopped to light a cigarette, as he moved on. Peter drove to the garage and got the car filled with petrol. He left it in the side street and walked back to his lodgings.

By ten thirty he was climbing the stairs up to his room.

He set the alarm clock to wake him at one thirty am and wound it up; he put the clock within easy reach as he didn't want it to wake the whole household when it went off. It had been a long day and he was dog tired. He settled down...and woke with a start at what seemed like two minutes later. He knocked the alarm off, the clock read one thirty. After a quick wash and getting dressed, he cautiously opened his door and listened carefully, all was quiet; he proceeded down the stairs, as he trod on the fourth step, it gave a loud creak, he stood motionless for a full half minute...

fortunately, all remained quiet, and he finally reached the front door; opening it and glancing outside, he went out and closed the door quietly behind him.

He found the night air rather cool after the heat of the day but was sitting in his car in no time at all. Driving through deserted streets, he was soon on the A580 with not another soul on the road. The speedometer was reading 120mph.

He wondered about Norah, in his own mind he felt sure that he had not killed her; he hoped not, he certainly didn't intend to, but things had become awkward and got out of hand and he had lost control. Would she be at Northrop and if so, was she on her own or would her sister be with her? Or had she gone to her sister's to stay with her? He would have to play it cautiously. Maybe the police are watching the place. "I'll park the car on the road and walk to the house," he said out loud to himself.

Before long he was at Wrightington Bar. He drove carefully down Carr House Lane. There were no cars about. He parked by the end of the driveway and walked up to the house. As it was expected to be, the place was all in darkness. He took the key and let himself in, closing the door quietly behind him. Standing in the darkness, he listened, it was as quiet as a graveyard; he proceeded towards the stairs and reaching them, climbed up. He arrived at the top and went over to Norah's bedroom door; by now his eyes had got used to the gloom, grasping the handle, he turned it and pushed the door, it creaked open, Peter froze, before opening it any further. He moved forward and to his immediate relief could see that the bed was made up and had not been slept in. This made things easier as there was no one else in the house. Going into his room, he quickly found a torch and a suitcase and put some clothes into it. He went round the house gathering together all the things he would need. By the time he was ready to leave he had two cases full and it was five minutes to three.

He closed the door behind him and walked back down the drive to his car, and drove back to Manchester. On entering the guesthouse, he went quietly up the stairs; when he got to the fourth step from the top he strode out to miss the step completely to avoid the loud creak that this step made.

Eight thirty am, Peter reached out and knocked the alarm off for the second time that day. He stretched and got out of bed, he felt grotty because of lack of sleep, but at least he had sorted things out and would be able to make good his getaway; at least, that's what he hoped for.

CHAPTER THIRTY ONE
Headline News

At the breakfast table conversation was not flowing in great quantities to Peter's relief. Roger folded his newspaper and placing it on the table, got up and looked at his watch. "Well, I'll have to be getting off; I'm travelling up north today. I may be back tomorrow or it could run into the next day, depending on how things go, so I'll see you all later." With that, he left the dining room and was gone.

Eric entered the room, "Good morning, Peter."

"Good morning, Eric."

"Have you no luggage with you, Peter?"

"Yes, I have; I left it in the car, I'm afraid I'd forgotten all about it, I'll bring it in when I've had my breakfast. I'll be going out on business today, I'll probably be back by teatime or thereabout."

"So you won't be having any lunch with us today then."

"No, no lunch for me today, thank you, I'll have something while I'm out."

As he left by the front door, he thought to himself, I can't use the car as the police may be looking for it; although Manchester was some thirty odd miles from Wrightington. But he could not be sure if he had actually killed Norah or not. Assault may be one thing but murder was something else entirely. The net would almost certainly be spread wider for murder. No, he would have to use public transport. Taxi drivers usually

188

have good memories and the possibility of being remembered had better not be risked.

Peter knew exactly where to go in the city centre; he made his way to Jonas Martindale and Son, Travel Agent and entered the shop.

"Good morning, sir, can I help you at all?" asked the young lady behind the counter.

"Yes, I think you can help me, I would like to book a flight to Canada, please."

"Certainly, sir, to which airport would you like to go?"

"To Vancouver International Airport, please."

"I'm afraid the only flight to Vancouver is on Thursday, sir."

"Is that the first available one?"

"Yes, I'm afraid it is, sir."

"Ok, just a single one way ticket, please."

Peter left the travel agents with his ticket.

His next port of call was to a local branch of his bank, where he deposited £6,000 in cash, and ordered an immediate transfer into his Swiss bank account.

On the day of the flight, at breakfast he saw Roger, the Commercial Traveller leave a newspaper next to his used plate. He went over and glanced at it – it was the Wigan Observer. Then to his horror, he saw a picture of himself on the front page and beneath it a caption that said:

'POLICE LOOK FOR ATTACKER'

Beneath the heading was a long piece saying who had been attacked and that the victim had been left with a severe stroke afterwards, and was unable to speak and was now in the Royal Albert Edward Infirmary, Wigan.

He picked up the paper – he needed to destroy it before Eric or Mary should see it. He folded it so the headline could not be seen and took it to his room. Tearing it up, he dropped the bits of newsprint into his rubbish bin.

He then went downstairs again to say goodbye to his host and hostess.

"I've decided to take a trip to the South of France for the sunshine – good for my health, the doctor reckons. I've got a bad chest, you know. So I'll be leaving."

"What, straightaway?" asked Mary, putting used crockery on to a tray.

"Yes, no time like the present. I'll perhaps send you a postcard."

"We'll be sorry to lose you. Don't leave it so long next time," said Eric.

"I won't!"

He went upstairs to pack his belongings. He then left the guesthouse and got the bus into the city centre and onto the airport.

Once there, after waiting what seemed like forever in a long queue, he checked in. His passport was stamped – he was on his way. He boarded the plane and settled himself in his seat. He heard the engines revving and sighed with relief. The plane began to taxi down the runway picking up speed. After a short distance it began to slow down and then stopped. The passengers all looked askance at each other. Why had this happened? Why had they stopped?

Ten minutes later, the door of the plane opened. Two men in plain clothes entered the aircraft and Peter felt a hand on his shoulder.

He looked up to see a stern-faced man who obviously would stand no nonsense.

"Are you, Peter Northrop?" He asked.

"Err...yes." Well, he couldn't deny it.

"I'm arresting you for the attack on Norah Gray. Will you come quietly?"

What choice did he have? He rose to his feet and handcuffs were quickly snapped onto his wrists. To curious looks from the other passengers he was led off the plane, through the airport to a waiting car.

"Get in," said the policeman.

He climbed in the back with the policeman beside him. His thoughts were in turmoil as the car sped through the streets of Manchester. So Eric and Mary must have seen the newspaper after all and shopped him. Unless, it was Roger; it could have been him. He didn't want to go to prison, be locked up for years- he couldn't plead 'not guilty' as there was a witness to his attack on Norah.

He was ushered into the Police Station and was interviewed by two detectives.

"Now, said Detective Inspector Brown. "Mr. John Peet has given us a sworn statement". He looked serious. "He states he saw you and intervened when you attacked Miss Norah Gray at Northrop House."

He was formally cautioned for attempted murder.

After this, he was then taken into a cell block, and a room on the left for processing.

This was a nightmare! The dismal room was bare apart from a table and chairs. He swallowed. "What happens now?"

"It's for us to ask the questions, not you," replied Detective Parks. "You'll be seen first by the flash-and-dabs."

Flash-and-dabs, what on earth were they?

He soon found out. Two police officers appeared and set to work. He felt demeaned being photographed and finger-printed.

Eventually, stumbling with fatigue, he was taken into the main block through a barred gate.

Keys rattled and doors clanged ominously behind them. He was shown into a cell for the night, carrying his cup, plate, knife and fork and chamber pot.

He tossed and turned on a hard pallet, kept awake by the drunks in the adjoining cells, cursing, groaning, and being violently sick.

The following morning he was driven to Preston, and the Crown Court, where, eventually he was in the dock.

"Are you Peter Northrop of Northrop House, Carr House Lane, Wrightington Bar?"

He replied in the affirmative.

The judge set a date for his trial. "Your trial will be held on Thursday, the 20th of November 1958. No bail will be set."

From there, Peter was taken to Preston Prison.

At Preston Prison Peter was given prison clothing and told he was a Category B prisoner.

This meant that he couldn't be made to work, but to relieve the boredom he agreed to do some work under supervision in the Prison library.

The other inmates were a mixed bunch from well-to-do's to nere-do-well. Peter befriended one man in particular; Reg 'Fingers' Coates, six-feet tall, dark hair sleeked back with hair cream, a scar down his left cheek, and the tips of two fingers missing from his left hand; a wealthy man who was in for forgery and money laundering. In conversation, Peter learnt that 'Fingers' was also due to appear in court on the same day as himself, the 20th of November.

Whilst in the library one day, 'Fingers' said to him, "I like you, Peter. And I am going to tell you something that you must keep to yourself. I've been planning a break from here, and if you wish I'll count you in."

"You're going to do what? How long have you been planning a break?"

"It's been planned for a while, and will take place on the day we are due to go to court."

"Who's doing it?"

'Fingers' tapped his index finger at the side of his nose, "Friends."

"But, how do you expect to bring this off?"

"It will be done when they are transporting us to court. The police vehicle will be ram-raided, and we will be rescued."

"But, what will happen after that?" asked Peter.

"Well," said 'Fingers', "I need an answer from you straightaway, are you in, or not!"

"Count me in," said Peter.

193

"Good! I needed to know because I have to get your paperwork done, new name, and passport and so on. I can't tell you where we will be going to yet as keeping that secret is of paramount importance, suffice to say it will be abroad."

Life in prison was hard for Peter as he had never been incarcerated before. He could not wait to get out, to have his freedom once more. The days dragged on; there was no one to come and visit him. He counted the days to the deadline.

CHAPTER THIRTY TWO
The Getaway

The day of the trial eventually arrived. Reg Coates went to Peter and said, "Everything's ready, your passport and other necessary papers; your new name will be Thomas Foyle, you'll get your stuff when we get away. You will be given instructions what to do then. You must carry them out to the letter, do not deviate from them for any reason. Any times must be strictly kept to. Do you understand, Peter?"

"Yes, I understand. And thank you, 'Fingers'."

"Good!"

"This break has to work; all we have to do is sit in the Maria and wait. The attack will obviously come from outside the van, and they will break in. Cars will be waiting to speed us away to a place already prepared for us."

The warders came for them at ten o'clock and took them from their cells in handcuffs and chains out of the prison building to a waiting police van where they were locked in the back and two policemen sat in the cab. The van set off for the Courthouse. In a quiet narrow road a Thames van with a heavy-duty towing bracket on the back was waiting. As the police van passed a junction an old Foden lorry pulled out behind them and followed them. As the police van approached the Thames van the lorry speeded up and rammed the police vehicle into the back of the waiting van.

All hell broke loose! Men wearing balaclavas covering their faces sprang from the lorry and the van and began to smash at the windscreen and side windows of the Black Maria with pickaxe handles. There was the sound of shattering glass, even though the windows were covered in wire mesh. Meanwhile, the men from the lorry were using a five foot crowbar and heavy-duty bolt cutters on the rear doors. While this was taking place, at the front of the van, bolt cutters had been used to cut away the mesh; the policemen had been dragged out and beaten up. At the back, the doors were burst open and the chains were cut from the prisoners with the bolt cutters and they were ushered from the Maria into a car which was parked in front of the Thames van.

The two policemen, barely conscious, were then shoved into the back of their own van and quickly tied up.

At that, the rest of the gang jumped into the Thames van and the van and the car sped away heading north on the A6. Just the other side of Fulwood in a quiet side street they abandoned the getaway vehicles and got into two different cars, ushering Peter into the back of one of them. They set off again, this time heading south taking a long route on the outskirts of Preston avoiding the A roads to by-pass the town centre.

Peter was impressed by the amount of thought and effort that had gone into the planning of all of this. There were even sandwiches and flasks of hot tea and coffee in the car so they did not need to stop so often on the way to where they were going; he had not been told yet where that was.

The other car which they had been following turned off at a tee junction. The rear lights flashed and headlights were flashed back. From there, they went on alone; Reg and Peter in the back; and the driver. "I can tell you now that our next destination is Surrey; Frogmore Farm, Leatherhead. From there we will be catching a plane at Gatwick Airport, you'll find out then where our final destination will be," 'Fingers' said. He then produced a packet of Craven A cigarettes and offered one to Peter.

Peter took it and they both lit up and inhaled with satisfaction.

"This operation must have cost a fair bit," remarked Peter, "disguises, a wagon and van, two cars, all the passports and paperwork, the men involved, the flights to wherever we are heading."

'Fingers' laughed. "I'm not paying for this with real money, you know."

"How do you mean?"

"I'm the best forger in the business, if I say it myself. Money's printed, not necessarily English and then it is laundered. You know what laundered means, don't you? Let's say we print one million pounds. We then sell it for say half a million. We've then got half a million pounds in genuine notes and whoever buys the false money from us distributes it. So that's how they make their profit, they make half a million, too. There are other kinds of laundering as well."

"That sounds good. If I wasn't in the lumber business, I'd come and join you," laughed Peter.

The driver put his hand over his shoulder and passed a large key ring with more than a hundred small keys on it, to Reg so that they could remove the handcuffs from their wrists. Although the chains had been cut with the bolt cutters the cuffs could not be. Reg tried each key in turn, after trying about seventy he found one that opened them. He handed the bunch over to Peter, the same key did not fit, so he tried the next one; on the ninth attempt, the cuffs opened.

"You're a jammy sod; you'll go a long way, you will."

"Yes and in more ways than one." They all laughed at this.

Almost seven hours later, weary from the journey, they finally arrived at Frogmore Farm. This turned out to be a smallholding, the farmhouse modest with a thatched roof. Nearby, were some small outbuildings where Peter imagined animals must have been kept at sometime, also a small barn.

Peter and Reg alighted from the back of the car. The driver then climbed out, he handed a key over to Reg; Joe then opened the barn doors and drove the car into the barn.

Meanwhile, Reg and Peter had gone to the front door. Reg took the key and opened the door and they went inside. A few minutes later there was a tap on the door. It was the driver. "I'm just off to my digs," he said. "See you later."

"Okay, Joe. Goodnight and thanks."

"Right, Peter, let's get out of these prison clothes and we'll throw them on the fire. I'll lend you something of mine for the time being, we are similar in build. My lady friend, Caroline will take your measurements and go out and get you some clothing tomorrow. Just tell her what you want."

Peter looked around; the interior of the house belied its exterior; it was like a palace; antique furniture Chippendale, old masters on the walls, gold plated taps in the kitchen and bathroom, Axminster carpets on the floors. On the dining room table was a bunch of pink and white roses in a lead crystal vase.

The front door opened and a beautiful young woman entered. She was five foot six, with long blonde hair. She had a curvaceous body and wore a low cut white velvet dress that revealed half of her bosoms. Dangling from her ears were gold earrings, and her fingernails were painted red. Her face was well made up, with red lipstick which matched her fingernails; she wore green eye shadow and mascara. She hurried over to Reg and threw her arms around him. "Hello, darling," she said. "It's good to see you."

"It's good to see you too, Caroline darling," he said, as they kissed passionately. Reg introduced her to Peter. "This is Caroline," he said.

Peter could see that she was at least fifteen years younger than Reg. He learnt later that Caroline had once been a stripper in a London nightclub 'The Blue Lagoon' until she'd met Reg.

"I'm sorry I wasn't in when you arrived. I'd been to the village for something for our supper. I then called into the Jug and Bottle of the Queens Arms." She took a greaseproof-wrapped parcel out of her shopping bag and opened it and showed them three large sirloin steaks, she then took out several bottles of beer.

Soon there was a delicious smell of cooking, which would be the first hot meal they'd eaten that day.

There was almost a party atmosphere as they ate the meal and downed the bottles of beer. After this, Reg produced a gold plated cigarette box from an occasional table. They each took a cigarette and Caroline placed hers into a long ivory cigarette holder.

"From now on I'll call you Thomas; my new name is Ivor Baldwin, and Caroline's is Lynn Redmond." Reg went over to a drawer in the sideboard and brought a cardboard box over to Peter. Upon opening it, he took out a passport and a visa, also in the box was a theatrical moustache, a small bottle of spirit glue, some other bottles containing liquids, and a small box which had a kind of greyish powder inside. Peter opened the passport and staring back at him was a complete stranger; although he felt that he could see something of himself in the photograph.

"That's Thomas Foyle, or was! He's no longer with us. He died in Ireland three years ago; and before you ask, no, he was not murdered, he died of natural causes. And you won't need to put on an Irish accent as he was brought up in England. When he was diagnosed with a terminal illness he wanted to spend what time he had left in the country of his forefathers, so went over to the old country. Tomorrow you will have your makeup put on, Caroline will put it on for you, she's an expert; she did all her own makeup when she was in the stripping business. Don't go out of here without it. You will have to become Thomas Foyle. The moustache has been trimmed ready for attachment. When you're done you should look just like your passport photo. I know you want to get to Canada, which is up to you. We will have to say goodbye then. In the meantime, when we get on the plane, you and I will be as strangers. Caroline will be going with me. When we reach our destination we will be safe then to get back together again. You will also be able to remove the moustache or grow your own. Well, I think that's it for now. Your room upstairs is all ready for you."

Peter slept like a log, exhausted from the day's travelling. The following morning, he rose, had a wash and a shave and went downstairs to find Caroline cooking a full English breakfast. "That smells good!"

Reg joined them and they ate a hearty meal.

After this the disguises were put on. Caroline went to work on Peter. She washed his hair, taking one of the small bottles from the cardboard box, she then applied some of the liquid turning his light brown hair darker to match the moustache. She then went to work on his face, attaching the moustache with spirit glue and reshaping his eyebrows with tweezers. After this, she took the small box of greyish face powder and applied some with a brush. She held up his passport as Peter looked in the mirror. He was astonished, the transformation was perfect. He was Thomas Foyle.

She then changed Reg's appearance in the same manner; the most noticeable change was that the scar on his left cheek had completely disappeared.

"We'll have to lie low, Peter, as we're waiting for a flight cancellation. Booking tickets in advance would be far too risky. Caroline will only disguise herself at the last minute as she's not wanted by the police, and is the only one who can go to the village to get food, or anything else we might need. These cancellations could be at any time now or could be several days away. We will receive a last minute call." He looked over at the squat black phone on the windowsill as if willing it to ring.

At last; three days later, the telephone rang. Reg picked it up. A broad grin spread across his face. "Thanks, Joe," he said, putting down the phone. He turned to the other two. "We're on our way. We have to be at the airport by five o'clock. Joe will be here in one hour."

If the appearance of Reg and Peter had been altered, the biggest change was to Caroline's appearance, the blonde hair had gone, replaced by a black wig, as had the dangling earrings. Her make up was more subdued. She was also dumpy, having put padding beneath her underwear. The tweed costume she was wearing could have belonged to a middle aged woman.

At three o'clock, precisely one hour after his telephone call, Joe knocked on the door. Reg opened it, "Come in, Joe."

"All ready?" he asked, handing over the tickets.

"Yes, we're all ready." He indicated the suitcases, and Joe picked them up and carried them out to the car.

Reg handed Peter his ticket. "Now, you'll know where we're going."

Peter looked at it. "Good Grief, we're going to Rio de Janeiro."

They arrived at Gatwick airport; opened by Queen Elizabeth on June 9th, with time to spare. Joe dropped Thomas with his luggage off at the entrance, and then drove on to a sparsely occupied area of the car park, where Ivor and Lynn alighted, took their luggage and made their way into the airport.

Thomas joined a long queue, eventually reaching the check-in-desk where a young woman studied his passport. She looked at the photo and then at him. He froze, she smiled, and stamping the passport, handed it back to him, along with his boarding pass. "Thank you for flying with us, sir. And have a safe flight."

"Thank you." He took his luggage and placed it on the conveyor and made his way to the Departure Lounge and seated himself. Later, he saw Ivor and Lynn enter the lounge who completely ignored him.

After some time had passed; over the Tannoy, a voice announced: 'THE 6PM FLIGHT TO RIO DE JANEIRO IS ON TIME. PASSENGERS

WISHING TO BOARD SHOULD MAKE THEIR WAY TO BOARDING GATE NUMBER TWO.'

Thomas glanced across at Ivor and Lynn; they showed no sign of moving, after a few moments he realised that he should go first. He got up and joined the people who were stood at the entrance, the queue lengthened, and then Ivor and Lynn came across. The gate opened and they all went into the tunnel leading out to the waiting aircraft. On reaching the top of the steps he was greeted by an air hostess. He handed his ticket and boarding pass to her and she tore off the counterfoil and handing it back, she said "Seat number nine, have a nice flight and thank you for joining us."

"Thank you," he found his seat and sat down.

Ivor and Lynn were in seats sixteen and seventeen.

After what seemed like a lifetime the hostess announced, "Fasten your safety belts, and extinguish all cigarettes, we are about to take off."

The engines roared into life. The fuselage shuddered; the pilot revved the engines and the plane moved forward towards the runway, the plane made a forty five degree turn, and began to taxi picking up speed. Then, it started to slow down, the hairs on the back of Thomas' neck stood on end. Was history repeating itself? How could such a well planned thing go so badly wrong? He could almost feel the hand on his shoulder. The aeroplane came to a stop. He felt sick. The pilot's voice came over the tannoy; "There will be a slight delay in take off, a small fault has occurred on the aircraft this should only take a few minutes to fix, we are sorry for any inconvenience."

Thomas almost cried out, "Phew!" That put the wind up me, he thought.

A few minutes later the aircraft began its taxi again this time into a steep climb up to the sky.

Meanwhile; back in England, Frank and Margaret Johnson had been discussing the release of Alan Kay due to insufficient evidence. Margaret was folding up some washing ready for ironing.

She picked up a pink blouse. "It's a pity I can't wear my gipsy blouse anymore."

"Yes, I liked you in that blouse."

"I saw Uncle Brett fiddling with that blouse on the washing line," piped up Oliver, who was playing with his 'Dinky' toys on the floor.

"Don't you mean, Peter?" His mother asked.

"No, it was Uncle Brett."

"When did you see 'im?" Frank asked.

"It was on the same day that Uncle Brett brought me home after losing his key. You and Uncle Brett had gone into your workshop and I was playing outside when Uncle Brett came out. He went across to the clothes line and was fiddling with Mummy's blouse."

"Did he see you?"

"No."

"Did he take anything from the blouse?"

"I didn't see him take anything, but he had his back to me. Soon after that Alice came to the back door."

"Did you see her take anything from the line?"

"No, she went into the house, and I went to play round the other side of the workshop. I didn't see her again."

Frank turned to Margaret. "Well, what do you think?"

"I don't know what to think," she replied.

CHAPTER THIRTY THREE
Welcome To Rio

During the flight lasting about twenty three hours, Ivor and Lynn continued to ignore Thomas completely and he ignored them. As the airplane neared the airport, a voice over the Tannoy advised everyone to reset their watches to Rio time 2pm.

The plane finally touched down on the runway at Rio de Janeiro, reaching its final destination on the apron, it came to a halt. And what seemed like an hour to Thomas but was actually only about twenty minutes; before the aircraft doors were opened and people began to alight. The throng made its way into 'arrivals' and collected their luggage. As they reached the desk a Customs Officer asked, "Anything to declare?"

Ivor and Lynn said, "No, nothing to declare," as they handed over their passports and visas.

But Thomas wondered if that was true in Ivor's case, as the man put a chalked cross on each of their suitcases.

As Ivor and Lynn left 'arrivals' the heat hit them.

A swarthy man appeared and approached Ivor. "Mr Baldwin?"

"Yes."

"I'm Pedro Santos, your driver. The car is waiting for you." He took a suitcase in each hand and trotted off with them. They followed to where the limousine was waiting. Pedro opened the doors for them and they got into the car.

Fifteen minutes later, Thomas came out. Pedro approached him, having recognised him from the description given to him by Ivor. He took him and his luggage to the car, Thomas got in. Pedro then put the entire luggage into the boot, got into the driver's seat, and they drove off.

"Right," said Reg, "we can use our own names now, unless any officials ask us about ourselves."

"I understand," said Peter.

"Good!"

They drove through busy streets, high rise buildings on either side, with the odd palm tree growing out from the pavements. The limousine made its way south, finally arriving at Ipanema and stopped outside a beautiful white villa not far from the beach. Pedro took their luggage into the villa and handed the keys over to Reg. The villa was spacious with balconies on the upper floors, marble and polished exotic hardwood floors throughout the building and a large swimming pool outside.

Life in Rio would be good, thought Peter, but he wanted to get back to Canada as soon as he could to sell the lumber business.

They all quickly settled into their new way of life. Sometimes going out together, sometimes Peter would go out by himself.

One day while they were lounging by the pool, Reg said to Peter, "I know you want to get back to Canada as soon as you can, but if I were you, I would wait a while, and let the hue and cry die down as they'll know back in England that you had been living in Canada and may well have informed the authorities over there about you."

"Yes, I do understand what you are saying, Reg, and you could be right, but it's a chance I have to take."

"Well, just in case you change your mind; I was thinking about opening a nightclub here and have been looking for something suitable, and I think I've found it. It's a bit of a rundown joint called 'Fernando's Place'. But it will be refurbished and renamed 'The Green Parrot' and I would like you to manage it for me."

At that moment, Caroline, wearing a skimpy bikini came out with some cold drinks for them.

"Thank you, Caroline," Peter said, he was scarcely able to keep his eyes from her heaving bosom. He really fancied her, but if he tried anything on and she did not respond favourably, he would be in trouble with Reg whom Peter thought was capable of anything, and might even have him shot if he ever found out.

They were interrupted by the appearance of Gabriela Carvalho the Brazilian maid, who did all the cooking and cleaning. "I'm off, Senhor; I come tomorrow to do your work again."

"That's fine, Gabriela, thank you," replied Reg. He turned to Peter, "you know, Peter, if you want to go back to Canada as yourself, I think you should at least grow a moustache so your passport photo will not show you as you were in England in case the police are still watching for you."

"Ok, Reg, I'll take your advice on that."

"Good, as soon as it's grown we'll get your passport made up. Would you like to come with me to see the nightclub? I'd be glad of your input about it."

"Yes, I don't mind going with you, when do you want to go?"

"We can go after lunch, if you like."

"Yes, that's ok with me."

Reg picked up the phone, and spoke to Pedro. "Bring the car round in two hours, will you, Pedro?"

After lunch the limousine stopped outside the villa bang on time. They drove north to the outskirts of Ipanema and stopped outside of the shabby looking nightclub. Upon entering Peter was surprised to see workmen already gutting the place.

Reg never ceased to amaze him with the speed and efficiency of anything he did.

"You won't recognise the place after refurbishment," Reg said.

"How long will it take?" Peter asked.

"About three weeks, maybe just over, to do inside and out."

"So you'll want an answer by then?"

"Yes, before if possible so I can get someone else, if need be."

"Ok, I'll think about it and give you an answer before the three weeks are up."

"That's settled then, you know Peter if you wasn't going to Canada at all, I would offer you a partnership in the club."

"Well, thank you, Reg, that's very kind of you, but as you know I have to go to sell the lumber business."

"Yes, you do."

The work on the club made good progress, even ahead of schedule. Sometimes Peter would go with Reg when he went there. As it neared completion, Reg started to interview potential employees: waiters and waitresses, doormen, cleaners, strippers, barmen and a hat check and cloakroom girl. Peter was present on the occasion when Reg was interviewing for the latter. He called the next girl over and she sat down.

The moment Peter saw her, his heart began to race, beads of sweat broke out on his forehead. He had only felt like this once before in his life, over Christine Day. Christine and her father had been killed in a tragic car accident back in Canada.

"What is your name?" asked Reg.

"Cristiano Francisca Dias."

"What experience do you have, Cristiano?"

"I was hat check girl here before it closed down."

"How long did you work here for?"

"Four years."

"So you are quite experienced then?"

"Do you live far from here?" interrupted Peter.

"No, not far," she replied, smiling at him.

He smiled back at her. Something about her really reminded him of Christine! Peter could not keep his eyes off her, and she kept glancing at him with those piercing blue eyes, just like Christine's.

Surreptitiously, he looked at her left hand; she wore no ring on her third finger.

"Well, I think that's all for now. We'll let you know," said Reg.

Later in the day, another young woman was applying for the same job of hat check girl. Once again, Peter was with Reg at the interview.

"What is your name, please?"

"Maria Fernandes."

"What experience do you have, Miss Fernandes?"

"I worked at 'The Mango Tree' in Rio."

"Why did you leave there?"

"My mother was diagnosed with a terminal illness and I had to give up my job to look after her; she died."

"I'm sorry to hear that. Well, then, how long did you work there?"

"I worked at the 'Mango Tree' for about seven years."

"I think that's all for now, thank you, we will let you know," said Reg.

He and Peter shook hands with her, and she left.

Peter had bought himself a car and made sure that from now on he would be present at all the future interviews, which pleased Reg, as he appreciated Peter's opinion.

After interviewing for the rest of the staff, which they had both agreed to, Reg and Peter could not agree on Maria Fernandes, or Cristiano Dias, for the hat check job. Reg put up his side of the argument; "Maria has had more experience than Cristiano, and further more, 'The Mango Tree' is a very popular high class club."

Peter had his own personal reasons for wanting Cristiano, and putting up the weaker side of the argument remarked, "Cristiano has had four years experience in this former club and she knows the local clientele."

"I know why you want Cristiano," chuckled Reg, "But I still think Maria would be the best choice."

"Well, I'll tell you what I'll do with you, Reg, if you'll put Cristiano in, I will stay on here as manager, but I will still have to go to Canada at a later date once the club is established; and to give us time to get someone else in as manager whilst I go."

"It's a deal," said Reg, shaking hands with Peter.

That night, Reg, Caroline and Peter went down onto Pepe beach and partied into the early morning. After a few hours sleep, Peter and Reg went once more to the club which was almost completed. The outside was finished; the front was painted pink with a huge green parrot in the form of a neon sign with the words, 'The Green Parrot' underneath, so it looked like the parrot was perched on them. The inside was almost completed too. They spent the rest of the day sending out letters to successful candidates for jobs, telling them when to start work; and booking entertainers, musicians, and a compere etc.

Three days later, and it was opening night. Peter and Reg wearing evening suits, complete with dicky bows, Caroline looked the part in a green satin evening dress which had diamante on the bodice that glittered as she moved. She had a diamante headband keeping back her long wavy blonde hair. And in her ears she wore dangling earrings that matched the headband.

Peter was busy organising the staff, learning as he went along. Opening time arrived at last; the neon sign was lit up outside and all the carioca's (locals) poured in wanting to see what their newly opened nightclub was like. While Reg and Caroline sat down to enjoy the floor show.

For the occasion, Reg had organised a specialist act, a Carmen Miranda lookalike. He had heard about Alana Lopez from the housekeeper at the villa, Gabriela Carvalho. She had been to see her in a show and had been much impressed.

There was a loud drum roll. The compere announced, "Miss Carmen Miranda."

Everyone waited in anticipation. She appeared to enthusiastic cheers and applause. She was a beautiful young woman. On her head, she wore a towering replica of the fruit bowl headdress, consisting of artificial oranges, apples, bananas and grapes. She was wearing a revealing costume in the style of a red satin top that was tied beneath her bosom and had different colour shoulder frills. The white skirt was open at the front with frills that matched the top. She began to sing the famous Carmen Miranda song:

"I,Yi,Yi,Yi,Yi, I like you very much
I,Yi,Yi,Yi,Yi, I think you're grand
Why,Why,Why, is it when I feel your touch

My heart starts to beat, to beat the band."

Her voice was as musical as a tinkling stream, and as she sang, she swayed in time to the music, revealing shapely legs, and very high-heeled shoes.

The song finished to applause loud enough to raise the roof.

Peter was keeping his eye on the staff. Something he would be doing over the next, probably two or three weeks. The idea behind this strategy was to find someone to take over the management while he was away in Canada.

He went over to Cristiano in the hat check, "are you all right," he asked?

"Yes, I'm fine, thank you, it's almost like I've never been away." She smiled.

"That's good; don't hesitate to ask if you want anything at all. I have never managed a nightclub before so perhaps you can teach me something."

She laughed, "What's to teach?"

"Well, for example, what do you do now that the club is full and no one is coming in?"

Again she laughed. "It doesn't work quite like that; people come and go all the time."

Peter already knew this and was just making conversation. Anything so he could keep talking to her.

The longer he remained in her company, the more he could see Christine in her. There was no doubt about it; he had fallen in love with her.

He was curious about her having no ring on her ring finger, did she have a boyfriend? He would have to ask her point blank. "I hope you don't mind me asking such a personal question but are you courting, Cristiano?"

Once again that beautiful smile appeared on her face. "I was; up to a month ago, but not now."

"Why, what happened?"

"I found out he was seeing another woman as well as me. So I told him where to go."

Peter breathed a sign of relief. "How will you get home from here?"

"I'll take a taxi."

At that moment one of the bar staff came to him with some problem. "I'll see you later, Cristiano, ok."

The barman and Peter went off to sort out the problem. Shortly after, the problem was solved and he went back to the hat check. Cristiano was just seeing to a customer; when he had gone Peter, approached her and asked, "Can I run you home when we close, it will save you your taxi fare?"

"Would that not be too much trouble?"

"No, absolutely no trouble at all."

"In that case, thank you kind sir."

Peter wanted to take her into his arms but he would have to be patient.

The club was in full swing and was a great success. By the end of the night clientele had commented favourably saying what a different club it was compared to 'Fernando's Place'. Not just because it was newly decorated but the quality of the entertainment was far better. This pleased Reg no end. But then, everything that Reg did was always a great success.

As closing time approached, the club began to empty. Peter couldn't wait to be alone with Cristiano who had to wait until every customer had gone. Finally the last customer handed in his cloakroom ticket and left the club.

Peter said good morning to Reg and Caroline; then he too left the club with Cristiano who showed him the way to her home. After driving for about two kilometres, she said, "Turn right here, fourth house on the right. Will you come in for a coffee?"

"Thank you, I will." He followed her into her apartment. Peter sat down while she made the coffee. "You speak very good English, don't you?"

She smiled. "My father is Brazilian but my mother is English, that's why."

"Oh, I see."

"Have you been to England?"

"No, my mother was on holiday in Brazil when they met."

They gazed into each others eyes. "Can I see you again? Outside of work, I mean."

"Yes, I'd love that."

"I'd like to stay with you all night, except it's already morning. Perhaps I should go and let you get some sleep? I don't want to rush you into anything. Will you be free later today?"

"Yes, I was going to see my friend, Loren Melo; but I'll ring her and tell her I can't come because I've met a very handsome man."

"Well, if you can't make it, I would understand," interrupted Peter.

"Oh, don't worry, she won't mind, it will be ok."

"I'll come for you at two o'clock this afternoon. Will that be all right?"

"Yes, that's fine."

"I'll see you at two." He kissed her gently on her lips, to which she showed no objection.

CHAPTER THIRTY FOUR
A Fine Romance

Meanwhile back in England; Norah had come out of hospital and was living with her sister, Jane, who was looking after her. Her condition was such that although she hadn't got any worse her chances of getting any better were very slim indeed.

The hue and cry over the attack on Norah had abated somewhat. The police were still in the dark as to where the two escaped prisoners had gone, it seemed as if they had disappeared into thin air, and had probably gone abroad, but where to? Although the police had made inquiries to find out if Peter had got back to Canada.

***

Back in Brazil; Peter slept in late, and had just about enough time to grab a bite to eat, get ready, and go to meet Cristiano. He drove the two kilometres and pulled up outside of her apartment. He rang the bell. His finger had hardly left the button when the door opened to reveal a smiling Cristiano. "Come in," she said eagerly pulling him inside, reaching up she gave him a kiss on the lips.

"How are you Cristiano, did you sleep all right?"

"Yes, did you?"

"Like a log."

"Would you like a coffee?"

"Yes, please."

Peter drank his coffee and put the cup down. He turned to Cristiano, "would you mind if I called you Cris?" He asked with a pleading look on his face.

"No, I wouldn't mind at all, I would like that."

"Oh, that's good, Cris." He leaned across and put his arms around her and they locked in an embrace. He kissed her tenderly. "Shall we have a ride into Rio and walk along Copacabana beach?" He asked her.

"Yes, we can do that, if you like."

In Rio they parked close to the approach, walked down onto the beach and made their way to the shoreline. As they strolled along Chris took off her shoes and walked in the water.

"I have something to say to you, Cris."

"Yes?"

"I have to go back to Canada to sell my lumber business, and I would like you to come with me."

"Oh, are you only here on holiday?"

"No, I've been here for over three months; when I have sold the business I will come back here," laughed Peter, "I'm thinking of opening a high class hotel in Rio, I've already chosen a name for it, 'Ocean Palace', what do you think?"

"That sounds lovely; I'd like to go with you, but what about my job? Would Reg let me go?"

"Oh, don't you worry about that, Reg will get Maria Fernandes to stand in for you. He would like that, and besides that, you wouldn't need that job anyway because I've fallen in love with you, Chris."

"Ooh. I think I'm falling in love with you, too." Once more their arms entwined and they kissed passionately.

"Well, now, what do you say?" he asked.

"Yes, I'd love to go with you. How long would we be away for?

"As soon as the business has been sold we can come straight back here; maybe no more than a week or two at the most, why?"

"Because I usually go to see my parents at least once a week, would you like to come with me when I go to see them? I will introduce you to them as my new boyfriend."

"Yes, of course I'll come with you. When do you want to go?"

"What about tomorrow afternoon, will that be all right with you?"

"Yes, tomorrow is ok with me."

After another late night working at 'The Green Parrot', that afternoon, Peter went to pick up Chris to take her to her mother's in Rio. She was waiting at the door as he pulled up." Hiya sweetheart," he said.

"Are you ready to meet my mum and dad?"

"Yes, I'm ready to meet them."

They drove into Rio, Chris showing him the way. They parked the car and walked the short distance to her mother's apartment. She rang the bell.

Senhora Dias opened the door.

"Hello, Mum, I've brought someone to meet you."

"Come in."

221

"Mum, this is Peter Northrop, my new boyfriend. Peter, this is my mother, Frances."

"I'm pleased to meet you, Mrs. Dias," said Peter, offering her his hand which she shook.

"I'm pleased to meet you, too, Peter," she responded. "Please sit down. It won't be long before Lorenzo comes home.

Within half an hour Lorenzo Dias put his key into the lock and let himself in. Still good looking, despite being in his middle fifties, swarthy with black hair greying at the temples, and with piercing blue eyes, he was about the same height as Peter.

"This is my husband, Lorenzo; this is Peter Northrop, Cristiano's new boyfriend."

"Pleased to meet you, Peter," he said in rather good English, "so you're the lucky man; the first one she's brought home to meet us. It must be love, hey Fran."

Frances smiled, "Yes, it must be.

"Peter has to go to Canada; he wants to sell his lumber business. He then plans to come back here; and open a hotel. I am going to Canada with him; we should only be away for two or three weeks. I'll come to see you when I get back."

"About this hotel, Peter, are you thinking about buying one that's already built, or are you going to have a new one built?" Lorenzo asked.

"I would have to see if there are any ready built one's available, if not I would certainly consider having one built, rather than wait for one to become available as I intend to make my living from it."

"If you do decide to have one built I could help you quite a bit with that; as I have a lot of contacts in the building trade, and they could save you a considerable amount of money."

"Well, thank you, Lorenzo, I'll bear that in mind."

After dinner, Cristiano helped her mother to wash up; whilst Lorenzo and Peter discussed the hotel project. After this, it was time to go as they were both working that evening. They said their goodbyes and Peter thanked her parents for their hospitality and their blessing. They then made their way back to Ipanema.

That evening, Peter picked up Chris from her home and they both went to the 'The Green Parrot'. Peter was keeping his eye on the staff again so he could pick out someone to manage the nightclub while he was away in Canada. One man seemed to stand out from the rest; he was the head barman, Marco Santana. Peter called him into his office to interview him for the job. "I am going to be away from the club for a week or two and I'm looking for someone to take over as manager while I'm away. I've been watching you work and I've noticed that when people have a problem they seem to come to you for advice; And I've noted that the advice you give them has always resolved the problem. So I'm offering you the position of temporary manager. What do you say? It will be more money."

"But, I've had no managerial experience."

"Don't worry about that. If you ever need advice go and see Reg."

"Well, if you think I'll be able to manage and it is only temporary, I'll say, yes, and I'll give it a try."

"That's settled then."

Peter went over to the cloakroom to tell Cris. "Hi, I've just found my stand-in manager; the head barman, Marco Santana. So we can go and book our flight as soon as we can."

"We can go tomorrow, after work, if you want to, about two o'clock?"

"Yes, that's fine, Cris, two o'clock it is." He stole a quick kiss; and left the cloakroom. He could relax now, so he went and sat with Reg and watched the floor show, relating his good news to him.

At two pm, the following day, Peter went to pick Cris up, as before she was already waiting at her front door. "Hi darling are you ok?" He asked.

"I'm fine, sweetheart."

"Cris, you do have a passport, don't you?"

"Yes, I do."

"Great! Do you know of any good local travel agents?"

"Yes, there is a very reputable one in Rio."

"Right, off we go."

As they approached Rio, Cris pointed, "Turn right here."

He swung the car right and after a few hundred yards, she said, "Turn left here, the travel agents is just a bit further along on the right." Peter spotted the shop, 'RIO TRAVEL AGENTS'. He pulled up and they went inside. The shop was very busy, which gave them some time to browse around.

"Can I help you, Senhor?"

"Yes, I want two return tickets to Vancouver International Airport Canada, please."

"When would you like to go, Senhor?"

"We would like to go as soon as possible."

"There's a flight leaving Rio International on Friday at ten am."

"That would be fine, thank you. Right, Cris, let's go and pack our bags." Peter paid for the tickets and they left the shop. They spent two or three hours in Rio, while Cris bought some things for the trip, Peter paying for them, of course. They then had a late lunch, before going back to Ipanema.

The next couple of days went over without incident. Peter kept his eye on Marco giving him as much guidance as he could. He packed his things in readiness; and was up early on the Friday morning. He said his goodbyes to Reg and Caroline and thanked them both for all they had done for him. "I'll see you in a week or two, or at least, I hope to be back by then."

Reg had arranged for Pedro to pick them up and run them to the airport, which he did, in plenty of time to catch their plane for the long flight to Canada.

CHAPTER THIRTY FIVE
Return To Canada

Peter and Cris boarded the plane; he was not at all anxious. He knew that his anxiety would start when they reached Vancouver International. The worst part being going through Customs, he would put that out of his mind until they got there. The flight was uneventful and arrived on time at Vancouver. The old anxieties now flowed over him, but he kept it from Cris.

"Are you all right, Peter?"

"Yes, why do you ask?"

"I thought you looked a bit pale."

They reached the luggage conveyor and he lifted their suitcases off as they arrived; and took them over to Customs. Peter was trembling and beads of sweat were forming on his forehead. It was their turn at the desk. He lifted the luggage onto the desk and placed their passports in front of the customs officer who picked up Cris' passport, studied it, glancing at Cris; stamped it and handed it back to her. It was Peter's turn, the customs officer took Peter's passport and opened it, he looked at him and looked at the photograph, then back at Peter; whose face was so filled with terror that he need not have worried because he looked precisely like his picture. The officer stamped it and handed it back to him. While all this was going on, another officer was checking their luggage and chalked a cross on them.

They left Arrivals and went outside into the crisp Canadian air. "It's colder than I expected," Cris said, as she wrapped her coat tighter around herself.

"Yes," agreed Peter, "it is cold."

They walked to the airport exit. Across the road was a sign which read, 'THE CAR HIRE COMPANY' which Peter had thought was in the best possible position that it could be, to catch business from the airport. They crossed the road and entered. "We would like to hire a car, please," said Peter.

"Certainly sir, we have a wide choice, what would you like?"

"I think I'll take the Chevrolet Impala."

"A good choice, if I may so, sir, they're new in, what about this one, it's only been out once."

"Yes, I'll take that."

"How long would you want it for?"

"I don't know exactly, could be one or two weeks."

"In that case how about paying for two weeks, and if you bring it back in one week we will reimburse you the difference."

"Yes, that's fine."

"So there's just the paperwork to do."

Peter turned. Are you ok, Cris?"

"Yes, I've warmed up a bit now."

The man came back with the forms to fill in. Peter felt apprehensive again.

"What name is it?"

"Peter Northrop."

"And what's the address?"

"2604 Royal Avenue, Burnaby."

"Sign here, sir."

They went outside; someone had already brought the car to the front and put their luggage into the boot. They got into the car and Peter headed west on Grant McConachie Way. They drove for about ten miles, turned left onto Kingsway, and onto Burnaby. "The old house has not changed much since I was last here."

"It looks lovely," remarked Cris.

"Once inside, Peter set to work lighting the log fire. The house was cold as no one had lived in it for some time. "We'll stay here for tonight and set off in the morning for the lumber yard."

"How far is it to the lumber yard?"

"It's quite a long way; what I'll do is try to contact a couple of guys who have shown an interest in the business in the past."

Whilst Peter was getting the fire going, Cris had made some hot coffee.

"It will soon get warm when the fire gets going; in the meantime, I'll see if I can get hold of Matthew Martin and Daniel Clark."

He went over to the telephone. Next to the phone was an A to Z index. He looked under M and found Martin's number, which he dialled. "Hello, Matthew, its Peter Northrop...Yes, I'm back home again...yes, I'm ok, are you all right?"..."Good! Are you still interested in the lumber yard?...I'm going to sell it..."Oh, excellent! You would get a bargain as I want a quick sale. I'll be coming up to the yard tomorrow, or it might be the day after. I'll see you there, then. Goodbye, Matthew."

A similar call was made to Daniel Clark and he, too, showed interest in buying the business.

"Well, Cris, hopefully we will get a quick sale and we can get back to Rio. What do you say to that?"

"I can't wait, Canada's too cold for me; I'm used to a hot climate."

"We will be off early in the morning, it's a long drive, we may have to stay there, for a few days, to sort things out, but there is a log cabin. Don't be put off by the name; it is quite a luxurious place, built just off the lumber yard."

They were up by six am the following morning. Cris made up a flask of coffee for the journey. "We'll get some breakfast along the way as there's nothing in the house."

By half past six they were on their way. At about seven thirty they made their first stop for breakfast.

***

Standish, England

Elaine and Anthony had gone to see his Aunt Norah at his mother's. Norah had unfortunately made no improvement, and was unable to communicate at all. Elaine and Anthony were discussing the situation that had arisen from the release of Alan Kay. (Due to lack of evidence) and were pondering the possibility of Peter having killed Sandra, and Brett, too. They reasoned that

Norah must have known something, for Peter to attack her the way he had, but they had no proof as yet. Jane had just come back from the kitchen as they were speaking. "Oh, that reminds me, I ran into Margaret Johnson the other day. She was asking about you and Anthony; and she told me something that may be of interest to you. She said that the red silk ribbon had gone missing from her gipsy blouse, and that Oliver had said that he had seen Brett fiddling with the blouse on the clothes line."

"Well, we will have to see what we can make of that; it wouldn't hurt to go and see Margaret, remarked Elaine."

***

Canada.

Peter and Cris had been on their journey for about ten hours including stops, and had been climbing uphill for the last few miles, from the car they could see the forest on either side and were only about four or five miles from the log cabin. "We'll soon be there, Cris."

"Oh, good, it's really quite beautiful round here, isn't it?"

"Yes, it is."

Ten minutes later, Peter made a right turn off the road down a driveway to the log cabin. He went and unlocked the door and let Cris in. He took the luggage out of the car, along with the bag of groceries they had bought. "What do you think of the cabin, now, Cris?"

"I would have never believed it from the outside, all logs, but inside it is like a palace."

The plastered walls were covered with red flock wallpaper; the centre piece of the main bedroom was a four-poster bed with an ornate canopy over it, with red velvet drapes. The second bedroom was more modest, with a double bed. The furniture in the rest of the spacious cabin was antique and resembled the furniture she had seen in films set in the past about the French palace of Versailles. The floor was of polished wood, scattered with bearskin rugs.

It was not cold inside considering that there had been no heating on for some time. "We'll get settled in this evening, and I will contact Matthew and Daniel first thing in the morning."

Cris unpacked, and put the food away in the refrigerator, electricity being produced by a large petrol-driven generator, housed separately in a hut behind the cabin. Peter lit the wood burning stove so they could have a hot meal. The stove also acted as a heater and so the cabin was soon very warm indeed. After they had eaten Cris' delicious meal, they settled down together and enjoyed each others company.

Cris yawned. "Shall we go to bed; we have to get up early in the morning, don't we?"

"Yes, let's go!" He leaned across and kissed her and they went hand-in-hand into the bedroom, (let the reader use discernment).

The following morning, they were up early. After a wash and shave, Peter stoked the stove, which had been in all night, and Cris made bacon and eggs for their breakfast, after which, Peter rang his two friends and arranged for them to come at ten o'clock.

The first to arrive was Daniel. "Come in. Sit down; I'm sure Matthew won't be long."

"I think he's here now," said Cris seeing him, through the window.

Peter opened the door. "Come in." He introduced Cris to them. They all shook hands. "Right, let's get down to business, I am offering you a bargain for a quick sale; the price remains the same, as I said in our telephone conversations."

"Yes," they both agreed.

"The only problem is because you want a quick sale, it is almost impossible to raise that kind of money in the available time," said Daniel.

Matthew also agreed.

"Well, I envisaged this, so could you two work together as a partnership, that way you would only have to find half of the money each of the asking price?"

The two men looked at each other and nodded.

"Yes, we could, and we could manage to raise that sort of money, do you agree, Daniel?"

"Yes, I think we could."

"So can we shake on it?" asked Peter.

They all stood up and shook hands.

"If you can raise the amount, I will have my lawyers' draw up the documents as soon as possible."

232

"We will set to work raising the cash straightaway," said Matthew.

Two days later, Peter got a phone call from Daniel. "It's all systems go, we have got the cash," he said.

"Good! I'll get my lawyer on to it, this instant, and tell him to work double quick on it."

"Goodbye." He stabbed his finger down onto the phone rest, and released it, the dialling tone came on. He dialled the number of his lawyers; they also did all the legal work for the logging business and Peter used this as a lever, saying that he would recommend them to the new owners and that he wanted the paperwork by the following day at the latest, including his will; the details of which he related to Mr. Frazer. He would bring Matthew and Daniel to their offices, within the next two hours so they could start straightaway. They agreed to this. He rang Daniel, and told him to get Matthew and be ready as he would pick them up in fifteen minutes. He rang off, and gave Cris a quick kiss and said he would get back to her as soon as possible.

He picked the two men up and drove to the offices of his lawyers, RIDING and FRAZER. Mr Jared Frazer's secretary showed them into his office, where Mr Frazer took down all the necessary details of Daniel and Matthew. Because Riding and Frazer already worked for Peter and the lumber company, he had all the information that he needed except for Peter's signature on both the deeds of sale and the will, which the lawyer had already drawn up. Matthew and Daniel witnessed

Peter's signature on the will, and Mr. Frazer placed it into an envelope and handed it to Peter who put it in his inside pocket. Daniel and Matthew had their cheques with them made out in Canadian dollars. Peter signed the receipts for the cheques which he handed to his friends and they handed their cheques to him. He also signed the relevant documents even though they were blank; saying that he trusted his lawyer to complete the documents in his absence, and Mr Frazer gave him an affidavit signed by him to that effect. Peter also instructed Mr Frazer to keep the documents appertaining to him for safekeeping for the time being, and that he would give him further instructions later about where to send them.

"Well, I think that's all," said Mr Frazer. "My secretary will give you my bill and you can leave your cheque with her on your way out." He shook hands with the three men and they left his office. Peter went to Mr Frazer's secretary. She handed him the bill, and he made out a cheque for the fee, which included the fees for Daniel and Matthew.

Peter looked at the cheques that Matthew and Daniel had given him. He smiled; he had sold the business for a substantial but undisclosed amount and could leave Canada as soon as he possibly could. He dropped his two friends off where he had picked them up, shook their hands once more and wished them luck with the business, said goodbye and made his way to his bank. Once inside, he waited his turn, eventually he got to the counter. He pushed the two cheques under the grill with a trembling hand. "Can you put these into my account, please?"

The cashier took the cheques and filled the details in on her sheet. She turned the cheques over and stamped the backs. "Is there anything else, sir?"

"Yes, can you have the money transferred to my Swiss bank account as soon as possible, please?"

"Certainly, sir, there will be a charge for this service."

"Yes, that's ok."

"We will take it automatically out of your account."

"Yes, please do that."

She took a transfer form and filled in the number which Peter gave her for his Swiss Bank account. Pushing it under the grill, she said, "Sign there."

Peter signed it and pushed it back under the grill to the cashier, who duly stamped it and placed it to one side along with other transfer forms. "Will that be all, sir?"

"Yes, thank you."

She pushed his receipt under the grill; Peter picked it up and left the bank.

When he arrived back at the log cabin, Cris was waiting for him. "Hello, wonderful," he greeted her.

Hiya sweetheart, I had a man here asking about you today."

The colour drained from Peter's face, the police, he thought. "What did he say?"

235

"Well, it was a bit strange really; he just asked if you were back in Canada? And I said, yes, he just said, thank you and walked off."

"No name or anything?"

"No."

"Well, that is strange," Peter said. "Well, I've got some good news for you, I've sold the business and we can leave as soon as possible. Our flight is not due until the day after tomorrow, so if we leave now, we can be back in Burnaby by..." He looked at his watch. "Say, ten o'clock tonight, and have tomorrow to ourselves, to do whatever you want to do."

"Ok, shall I start packing straightaway?"

"Yes, you can, and we'll get something to eat on the way, ok?"

As Cris was packing, Peter came to her. "I can hardly believe how well it's all gone; I thought we might have been stuck here for quite some time." The words sort of put his mind at rest, but then he remembered what Cris had said about the man asking about him. "Cris, what did that man look like, the one who was here today?"

"He was a bit rough looking, middle aged, with a crew cut; he had a sort of accent, kind of, maybe, Irish. He was about five foot, six."

"Mmm, sounds like Jack Brady." He was a bit of a trouble maker, he thought.

"I'm almost finished packing."

"Good."

"I'll make up the flask with some coffee."

"Then we can get off." Peter knocked off the generator and checked that everything was ok to leave. He put their luggage into the boot of the car. He had a final look round. All he had to do now was lock up and drop the keys off at Daniel's. Then they would be on their way.

After a fifteen minute drive, they were outside of Daniel's house. He got out of the car and went up to the front door and rang the bell. Daniel came to the door. "Hi Daniel, I've brought you the keys to the cabin and other keys, they are all tagged so you'll know what they are. We are off now, so once again, good luck, I'm sure you and Matt will be successful."

Thanks, Peter, have a good journey."

"We will, so long."

He got back into the car and with a wave of his hand, drove off.

They had gone about five miles along the mountainous road which was downhill when he looked in the mirror and saw what he thought was a police car. All his strength drained from him, and he automatically put his foot down on the accelerator. The police car, although it was some way behind them, still kept up. He wondered if the man who had spoken to Cris was Jack Brady. And if so, had he reported him to the police? Peter put his hand into his inside coat pocket and withdrew the envelope, he turned to Cris, "Put that in your pocket."

"What is it?"

"Doesn't matter, just put it away,"

She did so.

His natural instinct was to go faster. He pressed his foot down harder, the car that was following them, speeded up too. By now they had gone two or three miles. What Peter didn't realise was that he was spending more time looking in the mirror than where he was going.

"Aren't you going a bit fast?" warned Cris.

Peter didn't answer her; he was still watching the vehicle in the mirror. He realised that it was closing the gap between them, his foot went even further down; the speedometer was reading over 80 M.P.H.

Suddenly, a truck coming from the opposite direction appeared from around the bend, and was well over the centre of the road. Peter only spotted it at the last second, and swung hard right to avoid hitting the truck, but lost control. He could not pull out of the swerve and their car went through the wooden barrier. Cris screamed as the car plummeted down into the ravine. The car ran wildly downwards, Peter pushed hard on the brake, this only made things worse, as the vehicle started to slide, twisting and writhing, it turned sideways and then lurched and turned over and over. The wheels got caught in a shallow gully, throwing the car upright. At that moment, Cris pulled at the door catch, the door flew open, and Cris was thrown out. The car turned over again, and rolled for the next thirty yards until it hit a tree and came to a sudden stop, upside down. The force of the impact burst open the driver's door, Peter falling half in and half out of the wreck. Cris rolled from where she'd come out of the car and came to a stop not far from the wreckage.

CHAPTER THIRTY SIX
The Return Of Sexton Blake

Up on the road, the truck driver had stopped and climbed down from his cab, and was peering over into the ravine. The car that had been following Peter had also stopped, and a young man got out and joined the truck driver. "Can you see anything?" he asked.

"Not much, I can see some smoke; it's gone down a long way."

"He was travelling fast, I tried keeping up with him, but couldn't. We need to inform the police about this," the young man said.

"And call an ambulance," added the truck driver. This is a well known accident black spot, that's known by the locals as Dead Mans Gorge, there have been a lot of fatalities here."

"It's aptly named," said the young man. "I'll go and see if I can find a phone." He got back into his car and drove off from Dead Mans Gorge, driving fast, as being a young man, he often did. He had gone about seven miles with no sign of a phone box. Approaching a right angled bend too fast, he lost control and the car skidded off the road and into a ditch coming to a halt some twenty yards further along, although he was shaken up, he was not hurt, and after a minute or two he was able to scramble across and open the passenger door, and climb out. He stood looking at his car, it was not badly damaged, considering; but it was stuck in the ditch.

He decided to walk along the road in the same direction in which he had been travelling, hoping to come across a telephone. He had been walking for some time and still there was no sign of a phone, nor was there any traffic on the lonely country road, which was mainly used by loggers. He carried on walking for two more hours, and then he heard the sound of a truck. It appeared, but it was going in the opposite direction. The young man flagged it down and explained the situation to the driver, who said, "Get in."

He climbed up into the truck and they drove back to Dead Man's Gorge. They stopped, got out and looked over the edge; they could just make out the car with smoke coming up from it. "Come on," said the truck driver, "let's go and find a phone." They set off once more, and had only gone about three miles when they came across a telephone.

"I went the wrong way," the young man said, "I travelled for miles, and could have found this one ages ago."

The truck driver picked up the phone, saying, "This is an emergency, an ambulance and rescue equipment are required immediately at Dead Mans Gorge, a car has gone down into the ravine. I can't tell you how many people were in the car at the time."

***

Cris had come round but was still dazed. She was full of cuts and bruises and her left arm felt strange, a sort of dull ache. She lay still for a few moments; then she began to recall what had happened. She looked around and saw the car with Peter sticking out from under it. She tried to stand up but felt so dizzy and sick that her legs buckled from under her, and she sank back down again. She tried again, this time crawling, with one hand and both knees, her way to the wreck. "Peter, Peter," she cried. He was just lying there motionless. He looked terrible, a big gash in his head from which the blood had run down his face. She could not wake him up, so she tried to pull him out, but try as she may she could not move him. She was exhausted and just sat beside him, weeping, holding his hand, and praying that someone, anyone, would come to recue them. She heard a moan and felt his hand twitch. "Peter!" She tried to shake him without realising what she was doing. He groaned and attempted to push the car off himself, without realising that this was impossible. After a few minutes, he had come round sufficiently to grasp what had happened, but it was all muddled in his head. "Christine," he said, "I never intended to kill you, or your father. It was an accident. I can't feel my legs."

"I know it was an accident," Cris replied, "you haven't killed me, and my dad is alive in Rio."

Although he was only semi-conscious, he realised that they had gone down the same ravine as Christine and her father, and that the rusting wreck of his brother's car, along with others, lay just a few hundred yards away. "I killed my own brother; he should have died in the car that's just over there, not Christine." He moaned, "I

241

slackened the wheel nuts, but Christine and her father didn't take her car that morning, but my brother's instead, because she'd told him that there was something wrong with her car."

"You're rambling, Peter; what are you on about?"

He moaned again. "I had to look for another way of doing it, the opportunity came at the party, I had to do a lot of work to achieve it, to make it look like suicide. My hatred for him: I can't bear it, can't bring myself to mention his name, started when we were quite young. He was always the one that won, he was the one who was top dog, always beat me in sports, in everything we did. At the school's sports day when I was seven, he won a cup for running – I was second. The painful memory of my disappointment has never left me, our parents cheering and clapping him, not me. That cup took pride of place on our mantelpiece for years. He always got the girls. Christine was the only one I ever loved, until I met you, Cris. You are so much like her, please don't be offended. There were others in the past, but they meant nothing to me. I didn't think I could ever love again, until I met you. I love you, Cris, I'm sorry."

"Ok, lie still, I wish someone would come to help us."

"It was me who killed Sandra, not Alan, although most people would think it was him in the circumstances." Peter moaned, louder than ever. "She knew too much and wouldn't listen to me. I had to kill her, not that I wanted to. And

Norah, I didn't want to attack her, she'd discovered what was going on, I didn't know at the time if I'd actually killed her or not, I only found out later that she had survived, but suffered a severe stroke, poor Norah, she didn't deserve what I did to her, but I couldn't let her live knowing what she did."

"I can't believe what you are saying, Peter, you're delirious, you must be imagining all this, it can't be true."

"I'm sorry, Cris, but it is."

"And who's Sandra and Norah?"

"Norah was my brother's housekeeper. We have known her since we were boys; she was always good to us. I didn't want to kill her."

"You didn't kill her, Peter."

"No, but I may as well have done, she suffered a massive stroke, at my hands," and she didn't do anything wrong."

"And Sandra, who was she?"

"She was my...my..." at that moment he lapsed into unconsciousness. Cris got hold of him and started to shake him again, but soon realised that it was of no use, and took him into her arms and caressed him. "I don't believe you could have done all those terrible things, you're just fantasizing, but even if you had done them, I love you, and you love me, and the most important thing is our future life together, not the past." She made up her mind, she couldn't just sit waiting for help to come, she could now smell gasoline; she'd have to go and see if she could climb out of the ravine, which was an impossible task. She released him from her embrace, and crawling on one hand and both knees, moved slowly away from the car.

***

Standish, England.

Anthony and Elaine had arranged with their respective employers, to take their annual holidays at the same time. They had been putting two and two together. "We need to get back to Northrop House to see John Peet, we need to have a look in Norah's sitting room and Peter and Brett's bedrooms, if he'll allow us to," said Elaine.

"We'll go after lunch if you want to."

"Yes, we should catch him in, unless he's gone to the foundry."

They turned into the driveway at Northrop House. John's car was parked in front. "Good, he's in," remarked Anthony.

They rang the bell although Anthony still had the latchkey that his Aunt Norah had given him, but thought it rather cheeky to just walk in.

John opened the door. "Hello, come in," he said.

"Nice to see you again, John," Elaine said, with a smile.

"Nice to see the both of you, how's your Aunt Norah?" he asked Anthony.

"She's no better," he answered.

"That's a shame."

"John, would you mind if we had a look in Brett's study and also Brett and Peter's bedrooms?" asked Elaine.

"No, not at all, feel free."

"And Aunt Norah's sitting room?" added Anthony.

"Yes, help yourselves."

"Thanks, John."

"Where shall we start?"

"Let's look in the bedrooms, first, Ant," said Elaine.

They went upstairs and opened the door to what had been Brett's bedroom. They searched through drawers and cupboards; Norah had put a lot of Brett's things back that they knew had been in his study, his handkerchief, cigarette case, wallet, glasses, etc. "Well, there's nothing here that we haven't already seen," Anthony said.

"No," agreed Elaine, "let's go and look in the room that Peter stayed in."

They opened the door and went inside, a quick look around told them that most of his belongings had been removed, there were no suitcases, and hardly anything else. "I wonder if John knows anything about this, perhaps Aunt Norah has cleared it out?"

They went downstairs again and asked John if he knew where Peter's things had gone.

"No, I didn't know that anything was missing, he certainly didn't take anything with him the day he ran out of here after his attack on Norah."

"Then the only thing that can have happened is that he came back for them later," commented Elaine.

"What next, the study, or Aunt Norah's sitting room?"

"We'll look in the study first."

On entering the study you would never have guessed that a murder had been committed in there. Everything was clean and tidy. "You can see that Norah's been in here, all right."

"Yes, replied Anthony. They looked in the desk drawers, nothing of any use. The same for the tallboy, the filing cabinet only contained files. The cupboard with the double doors was locked, and there was the safe.

"We could do with getting into that. We shall need a locksmith," said Elaine.

"That'll cost a fortune," said Anthony.

"Oh, put it down to expenses."

"What! I'm not working officially on this case," he said.

"We might be missing something important if we don't look in there," Elaine insisted. "I'll get a locksmith if you have to pay for it yourself," she said with that cheeky smile on her face.

"I'm not paying for it, my middle name is Scrooge," retorted Anthony.

They left the study and went back into John's office. "Do you have a telephone directory?" she asked.

He handed it over to her. "Would you mind if we got a locksmith to open Brett's safe?"

"That's ok by me."

She found the number for a local locksmith. "Can I use your phone?"

"Certainly," replied John.

Elaine dialled the number. From the other end of the line a male voice said, "Hello."

"Good afternoon, perhaps you can help me? Do you open safes, it's locked, and the key to it has gone missing?"

Over the line, came his answer. "Yes, we can, what make of safe, is it?"

"It's a Pentagon safe," she replied.

"We charge by the hour."

"How long will it take you to open the safe?"

"A Pentagon safe could be up to three hours."

"How much an hour do you charge?"

"Five shillings an hour, madam," came back the reply.

"Good grief, Scrooge will have a fit!"

Anthony glared at her at being called Scrooge.

"Can you hold the line, please," she said, putting her hand over the mouthpiece, turning to Anthony. "He charges five shillings an hour."

"How long will it take?" he asked.

"It could be up to three hours."

"That would be fifteen shillings."

"Well, it's important."

"Yes, and it could be empty."

Elaine took her hand from the mouthpiece. "The safe's at Northrop House, Carr House Lane, Wrightington Bar. How soon can you come?"

"I'm free at the moment. I'll come straightaway."

"See you in a little while." She put the phone down. "Well, Anthony, while we're waiting for the locksmith, we'll go and look in your Aunt Norah's sitting room."

Norah's sitting room was just as she had left it. They looked in all the cupboards and drawers. On a shelf behind a trinket box Anthony found the pair of glasses. "Look at these, Sexton."

"They're Brett's glasses," she remarked.

"Yes, but look closely at them."

She took them from his hand and looked at them. She held them up and looked through them. "They've got plain glass in them," she said.

"Yes, do you remember going to the study when Brett was laid out on the floor, you mentioned his glasses and I said that he had a spare pair in his coat pocket which we did not examine closely?"

"Yes, I remember."

"Well, I think these are the same pair, but Brett could not see with these on, his eyesight was terrible; so what are they for?"

Well, perhaps Peter was putting them on so he could masquerade as Brett."

Mmm, maybe you've got something there."

The door bell ringing brought John from his office. It was the locksmith, a middle aged man with greying hair. "Come in." He showed him into the study.

"Oh, it's one of them, a PR830." He scratched his head, "One of their top models."

Elaine and Anthony came into the study. "Hello."

248

"Hello, are you the young lady I spoke to on the phone?"

"Yes, I am."

"I was just saying this Pentagon safe is a top of the range model, fitted with a very good quality lock, it may take some getting into."

"Oh, no," Anthony groaned.

"Shut up, Scrooge."

"I'll do my best, but I can't guarantee a satisfactory result."

"We'll, leave you to it then."

In John's office, Elaine was asking John if he knew anything that might help. They told him about the glasses.

"Well, Brett had me make an appointment to see his optician, David Bird."

"Do you have the optician's address?" asked Elaine.

He gave her the address.

"Do you know anything else?"

"Not really, he went for a dental check-up but that's all."

"Have you any idea what might have happened to the safe key, John."

"No, I've no idea."

"So we have to assume that Peter has it with him," remarked Elaine.

"If that's so, then we also have to assume that coupled with the glasses, Peter was trying to pass himself off as Brett for some reason or other," put in Anthony.

"Well, yes, I suppose so, but why?"

"That's something we don't know yet," concluded Anthony.

The three hours went over quickly and the locksmith came into John's office. "I'm afraid I haven't opened it yet, but I'm almost there, I should be able to do it before the next hour is up. Do you want me to carry on?"

"No," said Anthony.

"Yes, carry on," Elaine said, overruling him.

They all went back into the study, sticking out of the lock were seven or eight lever-like things. "I've almost got it," the locksmith said.

"Carry on, the boss said." And with that, they left the study.

Thirty-five minutes later, the locksmith came back to the office, "I've cracked it."

"Is it open?" asked Elaine.

"Yes, it's open."

"How much do we owe you?"

"Call it seventeen and six."

"Have you got the money, Anthony?"

Reluctantly, he handed the locksmith precisely seventeen shillings and sixpence."

"Thank you."

"Thank you," said Elaine with a smile.

John escorted the locksmith to the door. "You know, you have a very good quality safe there, which is useless without a key, if you like I can take the lock with me and make you a new key. It will only cost you nineteen and three, and in a couple of days I'll come back and put the lock back on the safe door."

"Yes, ok."

They went back to the study, where Anthony and Elaine were examining the contents of the safe. Amongst other things they found: a dental record, a small white pillbox, but most importantly, the red silk ribbon from Margaret Johnson's gypsy blouse. "Just look at this!" Elaine picked up the red ribbon and pulled it through her fingers. "I'll bet the fibre I found on the bolt matches this. Look!" On the edge of the ribbon was a frayed place, where something had snagged on it. "Can we take these items, John?"

"Yes, have you finished with the safe?"

"Yes, thank you. Can you let me have the address of Brett's dentist?"

"Yes, I'll get it for you in a minute."

The locksmith removed the lock from the safe door, and put it in his bag. He said goodbye to everyone, and John escorted him once more to the door.

He returned to his office and found the dentist's address for Elaine.

They said goodbye to John and left Northrop House.

"Right, Anthony, let's go to Preston and see if we can find this dentist and we can get something to eat whilst we're there."

They drove the twelve miles to Preston and went into a small restaurant, 'MATTIE and TISSOT'. After tea, they went in search of the dentists. They eventually found 210 Argyle Street and parked the car. Elaine got out and looked up at the name, 'WIL CAIN DENTIST'.

She stood staring at the sign.

"Come on, have you gone to sleep?" remarked Anthony.

They went inside and through a door into the Waiting Room. Two patients were sat waiting.

"Press the bell," a middle aged lady said.

Anthony pressed the button.

Joanne came in, "Can I help you?"

"Perhaps you can, could you tell us if a Mr Brett Northrop came here for some treatment, on, or around the 16th of July."

"Yes, I can," Jo said.

"That was quick," remarked Elaine.

"Well, it's a day I shall never forget."

"Why is that?"

She related to Elaine and Anthony the pantomime that had occurred, and that Mr Northrop's records had not been seen from that day to this.

"Are these his records?" Anthony asked, producing them.

Joanne took them from him and looked at them. "The label's been removed, there's no name on them."

"Is there any way of knowing who this file belongs to?"

"Well, if you care to wait until we have seen to our patients, perhaps we could check the dates of his appointments with our desk diary to see if they coincide," Jo said.

"We'll wait," Elaine answered.

"Forty minutes later, Jo was free. "Come through."

They followed her.

She opened the desk diary at the month of July and checked that the appointment dates coincided with those in the file.

"Yes, it looks like the file is Mr Northrop's."

"Do you remember if he wore glasses?"

"No, I can't be sure about that."

"Ok, thank you for your time."

They left the dentist's and Elaine stood outside and looked up once again at the sign, staring up at it. "There's something bugging me about that sign, and I don't know what it is."

"There's only one L in Wil," said Ant.

"Yes, but it's not that what's bothering me."

They got into the car and drove back to Standish. Anthony kissed Elaine goodnight, and they arranged to meet again the following morning.

It was nine fifteen am when Ant picked Elaine up. "Good morning, sweetheart, angel face," he grovelled.

She tapped a finger onto her watch. "You're late!"

"Sorry. We are going to D.A. Birds, aren't we?"

"Yes, we are."

They were soon on their way to Wigan to see Brett's optician. The policeman on point duty waved them on as they approached King Street, and they pulled up outside of No 121; over the door was a sign: D.A. BIRD OPHTHALMIC OPTICIAN.

They went inside, there were four people waiting. "Shall we wait?" asked Anthony.

"Yes, there may be a lot more in later," came the reply.

They went up to the receptionist and Anthony said, "We would like to see Mr David Bird, please, showing her his Private Detectives Identity Badge.

"He's busy at the moment; if you would care to wait I will fit you in."

One and a quarter hours later, and with three more clients waiting behind them, the receptionist was able to slot them in.

"Let me deal with this, Ant, ok?"

They opened the door and went through, to see David Bird. He was well built and six foot four in height, with greying hair.

"Good morning," Elaine said, "we'd like to ask you some questions about a client of yours, Mr. Brett Northrop?"

Anthony showed him his badge.

"I'm afraid I cannot disclose anything about a client."

"But this one's dead," explained Elaine.

"So you have a Death Certificate?"

"Well, no we haven't."

"I'm sorry but unless you can show me a Death Certificate, I can't help you at all. Bring me a Death Certificate and I'll see what I can do for you."

Anthony and Elaine left the optician's dejected. As they left the building, Anthony remarked, "That was a complete waste of time."

"Yes," Elaine agreed, "but you really can't blame him, he was only doing the right thing, keeping his clients' details confidential. I wonder if John has a copy of Brett's Death's Certificate."

"Let's go and see." Anthony started the car and they made their way out of Wigan.

"I've been thinking about those dental records. Why on earth would Brett want them?"

"Well, let's suppose it was Peter who went to the dentists that day, wearing the plain glass spectacles, masquerading as Brett, would he have any reason for getting his hands on Brett's records?"

"I can't see any reason why either of them would want them," remarked a baffled Elaine.

"Me neither," added the detective. All this has been very unfruitful."

CHAPTER THIRTY SEVEN
The Truth

They drove back to Northrop House. There was no sign of John's car. "He must be at the foundry," Elaine noted.

"Shall we wait awhile?"

"We can if you want to. I can't get that sign over the dentists out of my mind, I wouldn't care if I knew what it is about it, but I just don't know."

"It may come to you later."

"Yes, probably when I'm not even thinking about it. Shall we go and see if Granddad can help us?"

"Yes, we could be here all day waiting for John; he may not even show up at all."

Anthony started the car and had just moved off, when John's car came up the drive.

"He's here now," observed Elaine.

Anthony stopped and switched off the engine. John got out of his car and came over to them. "Hi, you two, what are you doing here again?"

"John, you don't have a copy of Brett's Death Certificate, do you?" asked Anthony.

"Brett's Death Certificate; no, I'm afraid I haven't. Why do you want that?"

"We need some information and can't get it without the Death Certificate," Anthony pointed out.

"I'm sorry, I can't help you."

"Well, we'll see you later, John."

"Yes, I'll see you again, goodbye."

Anthony started the car once more and drove off in the direction of Standish.

When they reached Doctor Hardman's they parked the car and went to the side door and rang the bell. "Doctor Hardman's housekeeper opened the door. "Hello, come in."

They went inside. "How are you two keeping?" she asked.

"We're fine," answered Elaine. "Is Granddad in?"

"Yes, go through."

"Hello, Granddad."

"Hello, you two."

"Are you ok, Granddad?"

"Yes, I'm fine, thanks."

"We have come to see if you have a copy of Brett's Death Certificate?"

"What do you want that for?"

"We need some information from his optician, but he will not tell us anything without seeing a Death Certificate."

"Well, I think I should have a copy of it somewhere. I'll go and have a look for it." The doctor left the room. He came back, a few minutes later, with a copy of Brett's Death Certificate, signed by him. "Is this what you want?" offering the document to Anthony.

"Yes, that's it," he replied.

"Thank you, Granddad; we'll let you have it back when we've finished with it."

"That's okay."

"You delivered both boys, didn't you, Doctor Hardman?"

257

"Yes, I delivered them both."

"Am I right in thinking that Brett was the eldest?"

"Yes, Brett was the eldest."

"How much older was he?"

"Oh, about five minutes, I think. Why do you ask?"

"Just curiosity," said Anthony.

"We'll have to make an appointment to go back to see David Bird, can I use your phone?"

"Certainly, help yourself."

Elaine dialled the number and accepted an appointment for later that day, at five o'clock.

"By the way, Granddad, do you remember giving Brett some sleeping tablets when we were in the post office?"

"Yes, I remember."

"Are these the ones?" asked Elaine. She took the white pill box from her bag.

Doctor Hardman took it from her hand. "Yes, these are the pills I gave him."

"Are they very strong or quick working?"

"Yes, both, Brett had suffered from sleepless nights for some time and he asked specifically for something strong and quick acting."

"We found them in his safe."

"Well, they are a dangerous tablet," the doctor replied.

"What exactly do you mean by dangerous?"

"Well, if you took six of them all at once, they would kill you."

"That is serious," remarked Elaine.

"So what would be a regular dose?" asked Anthony.

"One tablet; taken at night."

"And how many have been taken?"

"I gave him twelve tablets, and there are seven left, so he has taken five."

"Not enough to kill him if he took them all at once?" Anthony suggested.

"No."

"So what would be the result of taking four at once?" he asked.

"He would be heavily sedated, and definitely, falling asleep," said Doctor Hardman.

"So let's assume that Peter gave Brett four tablets in, let's say, a drink, so he could get the syringe with the insulin, into him, without any trouble. Does that sound feasible?" Elaine asked.

"Yes, that makes sense, without the tablets, Brett could have put up a fight," said the doctor.

"That's just what I was thinking," remarked the detective, "I wonder why Peter didn't just use six or more tablets to kill Brett?"

"Probably, to throw suspicion on anyone who could gain access to the insulin? He knew that there were quite a few people who would not mind seeing Brett dead."

"Don't forget, that if there were no obvious reason for Brett's death, there would have been an autopsy," remarked the doctor.

"That's true, but if the tablets were locked in Brett's safe; how could Peter get at them?" puzzled Anthony.

259

"That's a good question, perhaps we haven't got it quite right; supposing Brett took them from his safe, to take one and Peter took the opportunity, to take four more, before Brett had time to put them back in the safe. Or maybe Brett did not keep them in the safe at all, and Peter put them in there after he had killed Brett?" Elaine reasoned.

"Could be any one of those ideas, and we'll never know for certain," summed up Anthony.

At four forty that afternoon they set off to go and see David Bird. The traffic through Wigan at that time was quite heavy and the going was slow. They were held up by the policeman on point duty, for what seemed like an hour; when he finally waved them on. Turning into King Street they pulled up outside of No.121, D.A. BIRD OPHTHALMIC OPTICIANS it was five to five. On entering, they found David Bird waiting for them. "Good evening."

"Good evening," Elaine and Anthony answered in unison. We have the Death Certificate that you requested."

He took the certificate from her hand. "That looks to be in order, I'm sorry to hear he's died. What is it you wanted to know?"

"Did you make up a pair of spectacles, with plain glass lenses for him?"

"Yes, I did."

"But Brett couldn't see a thing without his glasses," stated Anthony.

"Did he tell you why he wanted them?" asked Elaine.

"Yes, he did."

"So what did he say?"

"He told me in confidence that he wanted to try contact lenses, in the hopes that he would have more success with the ladies..."

Elaine laughed. "From what I've heard he'd already had enough success with the ladies!"

Ignoring her remark, Mr Bird continued; "And I told him that he would have to wear them just for short periods to begin with, as he would have to become accustomed to them. As he got over the initial stages, he wanted to wear them for longer periods, but he said that he didn't want to be seen sometimes without his glasses, and sometimes with, until he had got fully used to the new contacts, and that is why he asked me to make the plain glass spectacles."

"Well, Elaine, it's a pity we didn't examine the two pairs of glasses more closely in the study just after Brett's death, to see which ones he was wearing at the time, isn't it?" remarked Anthony.

"Well, yes, I suppose so," Elaine answered.

"Thank you, Mr Bird. I think that's all we need to know." They all shook hands, and Elaine and Ant left the opticians.

"What did you make of that, Elaine?"

"I don't know what to make of it, what do you think?"

"Mmm, I wonder if that's why Brett was always locking his study door whilst he was in there, so he could put the contact lenses in without anyone knowing during the early stages," he said.

"You could be right."

"So on the night of the party, Peter must have been in there with him, having given him the sleeping tablets in his drink, and then injecting him with the insulin, after that he left the study and bolted the door with the red ribbon, from the outside, ok?"

"Well, on the face of it, yes," remarked Elaine. By now they had reached Standish.

"Do you want to call back at your granddad's to give him back Brett's Death Certificate or would you rather go home?"

"We'll call back at Grand's."

Anthony parked the car and they went up and rang the doorbell. Mrs Williams opened the door. "You're soon back."

"Yes, we are," answered Elaine.

They went through to the library where the doctor was reclining in a chair with a book in his lap. He looked up. "Come in," he said.

Elaine handed him the certificate. "Thank you, Granddad, we found out what we wanted to know."

"Oh, that's good."

"How long has Alice Bentham been on insulin?"

"Oh, let me see, it was not long before her forty first birthday, why?"

"I was just wondering how Peter got hold of it, that's all."

"I don't know."

"Perhaps I should go and talk to Alice.Right, Ant, you can take me home now."

"Ok, goodnight Doctor Hardman." He shook hands with the doctor.

"Goodnight, Granddad." Elaine kissed his cheek.

Anthony drove her home.

The following morning, Anthony pulled up outside of Elaine's house. He switched off the engine and waited. For once he was early.

Eventually, she came out. "My goodness, have you been up all night?"

"No, I haven't," remarked a bright and cheerful Anthony. "Where do you want to go to?"

"I want to go and see Alice Bentham; you know where she lives, don't you?"

"Yes, number 2, Church Lane."

"So what are you waiting for, Anthony?"

"I thought I might get a kiss."

She smiled at him, in that beautiful way that she had with her, and gave him a big kiss. "How about that?" she asked.

"Let's go."

And off they went to Wrightington Bar. Anthony turned left into Church Lane and drove the short distance, pulling up outside Alice's house. "We're here."

They walked up Alice's path, to the front door. Anthony knocked and waited. There was no reply. "Perhaps she's at the back, pegging out washing, or something," Elaine suggested.

They walked round the side of the house to the back, but there was no sign of Alice.

"Could she be at Northrop?" Anthony queried.

"She might be, shall we go and see?"

263

Anthony turned the car around and drove down to the crossroads and turned into Carr House Lane. A few hundred yards on, and he turned into the drive of Northrop House. There was no car on the driveway. "It looks like John's not here either, Anthony observed. "Perhaps they've gone out together?"

"Could have, I suppose."

"Whilst we're here, what about calling on Margaret Johnson, to see what she can tell us?" Elaine suggested.

"Yes, if you like, we can do."

They left the car and walked across the front of the house to the small bungalow. Elaine knocked at the door, which Margaret opened.

"Oh, hello, come in," she said.

They entered. Margaret took them through the hall and into the Living Room. "Do sit down."

"We wanted to have a word with Alice, but she's not home, and we thought she may be at Northrop, but there's no one in."

"Yes, I saw them leave about half an hour ago, gone shopping to Chorley Market, I expect."

Margaret, can you tell us anything about that day when Oliver saw someone messing with your blouse? Anthony's mother said she had bumped into you, and that you had mentioned it to her. And, I've got some good news for you; we have found the red silk ribbon from your blouse."

"What! Where was it?"

"We found it at Northrop House," said Elaine, looking at Anthony.

"Why, that's wonderful news, I have wanted to wear that blouse many a time, but couldn't, just because the ribbon was missing."

"So could you tell us what young Oliver said about it?"

"Yes, he said, he had gone out to play near the workshop, while Brett and Frank went into it to look for something to lock Brett's study door. After a while, Brett came out but he did not see Oliver because he was hidden from view by the workshop. Brett had turned left and gone to the clothes line, and Oliver came from behind the workshop and saw him fiddling with my blouse, but could not see anything else as Brett had his back to him."

"Thanks, Margaret, you've been a great help."

"When can I have my ribbon back?"

"Well, I'm not sure yet, but it will be as soon as possible. And thank you, once again, for all your help."

Anthony and Elaine left the bungalow and got back into the car.

"Where to now?" he asked.

"We may as well go to my home for a while; I would still like to see Alice, if we can catch her in sometime."

"Right, that's ok then!"

They reached Elaine's home and entered. At that time of day there was no one in. Elaine seated herself at the table, with her head in her hands; after a few minutes, she got up and fetched some paper and a pen and started to write: WIL CAIN DENTIST. She stared at it, and then she started to cross out letters and, as she did so, wrote them down again. After several attempts, she jumped up. "I've got it!!"

"Got what?" puzzled Anthony.

"That sign at the dentist's, it's an anagram."

"What is it an anagram of exactly?"

"Can't you see it?"

"No."

"It's an anagram of IDENTICAL TWINS. Oh, my God, Anthony, it's just dawned on me, we've been looking at this all wrong. Peter didn't kill Brett; it was Brett who killed Peter! Don't you see? Brett didn't want contact lenses for the sake of his womanizing, it was so he could remove his glasses and look just like Peter, putting them onto Peter after killing him. So everyone would think he was Brett locked in his own study, the door bolted on the inside. Norah must have cottoned on, and that's why Brett, masquerading as Peter, attacked her. We can't be sure why he killed Sandra, perhaps he told her the truth and she just could not cope with it, or maybe she just drew the line at murder and threatened to expose him, and so he had to kill her. It's all falling into place, it's a bit rough around the edges as yet but I'm sure I'm right."

"We'll have to go to the police with this, Anthony."

"Yes, we will."

"I still want to speak to Alice, as soon as I can catch her. I'll ring Northrop to see if they have come back." Elaine rang, John answered the phone and she asked if they could go down to see them?

"We'd be only too pleased," he replied.

Anthony and Elaine went to Northrop House and rang the bell. John opened the door, "Come in."

"I'm glad I've caught you, I would like to ask Alice some questions, if she doesn't mind; that is."

"I'm sure she won't mind, she's in the Living Room, go through."

"Thank you, John," said Elaine.

"Hello, Alice, how are you?"

"I'm fine, thank you."

"I would like to ask you about your insulin when you are at work?"

"What do you want to know?"

"Did you notice if any of your insulin was missing at all?"

"Yes, I did realise that an ampoule was missing; and a syringe too. But I was too frightened to say anything about it, in case I was blamed for killing Brett."

"Where was the insulin kept?"

"I kept it in the servant's workroom."

"When did you find it was missing?"

"After Brett's body had been found."

"Don't you think you should have told the police?"

"Yes, but I was too afraid. I thought I would be blamed, as I have said."

"Ok, thank you, Alice." She turned to John, "Do you know anything that might help?"

Well, the day after Alice had told me about how Brett had treated her so badly, he came into my office to remind me to make an appointment for him to see his dentist. I remember being short with him. He left my office, and as my office door was open I saw him go into the Dining Room, as you know, you can go through the kitchen and into the servant's workroom. I obviously could not see him do that, but he was in there quite some time before he came out and left by the front door."

"Well, thank you both, you have been a great help."

"Yes, thank you, your information will help us a great deal," said Anthony.

"Well, Ant, shall we get off now?"

"Yes, we'll have to go."

John showed them to the door and they said their goodbyes and left Northrop House.

"Well, Ant, that was an opportunity for Brett to get hold of the insulin, wasn't it?"

"Yes, it was."

"That's another piece of the puzzle that's fallen into place," said a pleased Elaine. "If I wasn't quite certain before, I am now. It was Brett that killed Peter, not the other way round. It is more than likely that Brett strangled Sandra and attacked Norah, too. I wonder where he is, and if he'll ever be found. And will he ever be called to account for all his evil acts."

***

Dead Mans Gorge, Canada.

Cris sank down on the ground, exhausted, her throat sore from shouting for help to no avail. She slipped back into a semi-conscious state. Later, she

268

slowly came round. She began to shout once more, desperate to alert someone to their plight.

All of a sudden, she heard voices and saw rescuers descending into the ravine on ropes and with equipment.

Her heart leapt. Elated, she turned and cried, "Peter! Peter! They're here, we're saved. Thank God! Thank God!"

She turned back to look again at the rescuers and was startled by a big bang behind her. She turned, to see a horrendous sight. The car had exploded, and from it, flames were shooting high into the sky. Finding a strength she didn't know she possessed she started to run towards the car, but was beaten back by the heat from the flames.

Sobbing hysterically, she collapsed, too devastated to realise that the rescuers had reached her.

They gave her a sedative and strapped her onto a stretcher, and she was hauled up out of the ravine and into a waiting ambulance, which took her to hospital, she having a broken arm, as well as a broken heart. The hospital management informed her parents, and a few days later, they flew to Canada and took a saddened Cristiano back home to Brazil.

She had only been at home for a few days, when she remembered the envelope that was in the pocket of the winter coat which she'd worn in Canada. She took the envelope out, and opened it. Inside, she found Peter's will; a will made out in her favour. Her eyes filled with tears at the thought that Peter should care so much for her, as to leave her all his money. With the will was a receipt for a considerable sum; and at the bottom of it was the address of a bank in Canada. Also there was a slip of paper with the address of a Swiss bank and a number on it. She got her lawyer to look into it for her. Needing a job to take her mind of her recent trauma, she went back to work for Reg at the Green Parrot as a hat check girl as Maria Fernandes was leaving to have a baby. Later, she started seeing Marco Santana who had been kept on as manager.

***

Some time later, John was reading the 'News of the World' and he came across this article:

BRITISH MAN DIES IN CANADA
Mr, Peter Northrop aged 39,
Originally from Lancashire,
England, was burnt to death
when his car, avoiding a
truck, plunged into a
ravine and later exploded.

Shocked, by this, he gasped, so Brett was dead. He showed the piece to Anthony, Elaine and Alan Kay, who said wryly, "So he got a good roasting, after all!"

John, who knew the full history of the Northrop's, he being one himself, wondered if there really was a curse on the family. If there was, had it surfaced again?

And as it is often said, history repeats itself!

EPILOGUE

Cristiano Dias.

Sometime later, she heard from a Swiss bank and received a cheque for a considerable sum, more than enough to build a hotel and furnish it throughout. This, she wanted to do as it had been Peter's plan for them to do together. She called the hotel, the Northrop Hotel in memory of Peter. Although she would always love Peter, she couldn't stay single for ever, and she married Marco Santana, and they managed the new venture together.

Reg (Fingers) Coates.

He went on to open another nightclub, and also to make an honest woman out of Caroline, with the fanciest wedding you ever saw. Rivalling, that of Aly Khan and the American film star, Rita Hayworth.

Norah Gray. Jane Hilton.

Norah made a slight recovery from her stroke; she could speak odd words, and got a bit of movement back, in her right arm, but never made a full recovery. Her sister, Jane, looked after her for the rest of her life.

Alan Kay.

He was completely exonerated of Sandra's murder, and later met a young woman and re-married, and became father to a daughter.

Dr. Hardman.

He retired from his practise and spent a lot of time in his library writing a murder mystery, based on recent events and happenings, sometimes asking his granddaughter, Elaine for her advice.

Frank Johnson.

He stayed on as gardener and handyman, at Northrop House, and lived happily with Margaret, Oliver and his dad, Bill. As Oliver, got older, he learned from his dad and became good with his hands. Bill lived on for a few more years, and then passed away peacefully in his sleep.

John Peet. Alice Bentham.

They were married and Alice, despite being over forty gave birth to identical twin boys. John; as next of kin to Peter and Brett on his maternal side, applied for letters of administration and claimed the foundry and Northrop House, which they moved into as their new home. John was now owner and managing director, and continued to run the foundry successfully.

Anthony and Elaine had been discussing their future together. "How about you and me forming our own private detective agency, Hilton and Blake?" he suggested.

"Blake and Hilton," she replied.

"What about Hilton and Hilton?" He asked.

"Now, that, I do like," she said, with that lovely sweet smile on her face.

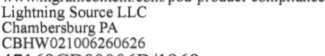